# Apple Tree

*Love, Betrayal And The Loss Of Innocence*

# Jessica Tilles

Xpress Yourself Publishing™
Upper Marlboro, Maryland

Published by Xpress Yourself Publishing™

P.O. Box 1615

Upper Marlboro, Maryland 20773

All Xpress Yourself Publishing titles are available at special quantity discounts for bulk purchases for sales, promotion, premiums, fund-raising, educational or institutional use.

Special book excerpts or customized printings can also be created to fit specific needs. For details, write to Xpress Yourself Publishing, P.O. Box 1615, Upper Marlboro, MD 20773. Attn: Special Sales Department.

ISBN: 0-9722990-2-5

For author appearances, contact:

A. Pierre Poinsett

Public Relations

The Poinsett Group

(312) 671-6757

apierresr@sbcglobal.net

Printed in the United States of America

Also by Jessica Tilles

Anything Goes
In My Sisters' Corner

For Mark

Timing is everything in this world.
You are right on time.

# Acknowledgements

I am going to make this short and sweet. Then, I will make a beeline to the fridge for my midnight snack. To my family. . .A loving thank you to my parents, Jesse and Wallace Wright, for your continued support and unconditional love. A huge shout out to my brother, Herbert Lipscomb; my sisters: Leslie Martin, Colleen Green, Sheila Wright, Jacqueline Johnson and Valerie Lowen; my nieces and nephews: Erika, LaToya (somewhere in Germany), Chris, Christopher, Paul, Kaleya, Brian and Antonio; and to Victor Tilles for challenging me three years ago and being a wonderful friend. You knew I had it in me before I did. To my publicist, A. Pierre Poinsett. Thank you for being my friend, my right hand, and handling all of my scheduling, thus allowing me to do what I do best, write. A sincere thank you to my editors, Carla M. Dean of U Can Mark My Words Editorial Service and Jo Hawley Chubbs for doing a wonderful job and for being two very dear friends. I wouldn't be where I am today had it not been for the following people: Jackson Mississippi Readers Club—Sherie Johnson, Mary L. Bailey, Dominique Ramsey, Kaisha Moss, Debra Fuqua, Deborah Terrell, Linda (Lynn) Johnson, Rita Wilkerson, Cassundra Course, Vestina Bailey, Dannette Mallard, Angela Thomas, Brenda Tillman and Linda Washington-Johnson—I love my silver gift; Michelle McGriff, author of *For Love's Sake;* Tahira Chloe Mahdi, author of *God Laughs Too: Incidents in the Life of a Black Chick;* T. L.

Garner, author of *Uncle Tommy's Cabin;* Karibu Books; Lambda Rising Books; Sisterspeak Book Club; Gary Johnson, Founder of *Black Men In American.com;* Writers Rx; A Nu Twista Flava; RAWSISTAZ; Book-Remarks.com; Lawrence Wayne, Founder, Memphis Black Writer's Conference and Film Festival; William and Glenda Barlow; Shari L. McCloy; Alfunzo and Teresa Clark; Greg and Jenise Dougherty and their clan; Robilyn Heath and the Girlfriend's Reading Circle; Lenox and Renee Coles, Darlene Stukes; Damita Shaw; the Tradewinds Crew: Jo, George, Montgomery, Amos, Fred, Wade, Alvin, Doreen, Sharon, Dee, Cocoa (the best bartender in the world—girl can make a mean Apple Martini), Dot, Holly and Greg (my sweetie); 2Spicey & HTJ Productions—when is the next cabaret?; all my sisters at the DC Licensing and Regulations Department; A Good Book and A Cup of Java in Memphis, Tennessee; Sister Malia and Caravan Books & Imports; Shunda Leigh, Founder of *Booking Matters Magazine*; Bruce Pugh who attends all of my local signings; my Southampton, New York connection: Louise Levy, Lorraine Ward (Aunt Pete), Audrey Gaines, Rosalind, Todd, Debbie, Gloria, Helen and the rest of the clan (way too many to shout out, but I love you all); my Emporia, Virginia connection: Lorraine Roberson, Johnnie Bradley, Lydia Calviness, Sadie Barber, Littleton, Rose and Angela Parker, Brenda Taylor and her folks; my Augusta, Georgia connection: Otis and Monica Moss and their clan; my Orlando, Florida connection: Chuck and Deborah Brown and their off springs – Hudson too; my Washington, DC connection: Dianne and Scott Robinson, Barbara Allison and Rick Jarvis,

Barbara Rose and Bob, Aunt Selma, Aunt Marty, Uncle Lee, Bernice, Kenny and Terry Rowe, Courtney Titus – keep writing cousin; my extended family: Daddy Claude White, Bently Dennis, Kim and Jimmy White, Debbie and Charles Thomas, Vincent and Wilma and their crew, Barbara Dennis and her beautiful girls, Morgan and Taylor, Michelle Tiggle and Miss Rachelle, Lenora Daniels (you're my Godmother too!), Dr. Denise Daniels, Kim, Chris and their handsome fellows and my newly adopted niece, Teresa (don't say I never include you!).

All right, I think that does it. To those I forgot, please write your name here _____.

Sincere thanks and continued blessings to everyone!

Jessica Tilles

# Author's Note

*AppleTree* is a work of fiction. Any references I have made to actual events, real people, living or dead, or to real locales are intended only to give the novel a sense of reality and authenticity. Other names, characters, places and incidents are either the product of my imagination or are used fictitiously and their resemblances, if any, to real-life couterparts, is entirely coincidental.

# Apple Tree

# Chapter 1

Jalisha and Corine peeped through the crack of their bedroom door and watched as their mother's head bobbed back and forth, in a circular motion, into the abdomen of a man they had never seen before.

"What is she doing?" asked eight-year-old Corine. "Why is her head moving like that?"

"Hush. Do you want her to hear you?"

The sisters observed as their mother worked her fifth trick of the night.

"Is she almost done?" Corine asked.

"Looks like it," Jalisha guessed.

"Lisha, how can you tell?"

"How can I tell what?" Jalisha snapped, totally annoyed at what was taking place before her.

"That she's almost done."

"His legs look wobbly."

"Oh. . ." Corine trailed off with a look of confusion on her face.

Jalisha was right. The man's knees buckled and his head tilted back as he expelled a deep, hearty moan from his esophagus. A white liquid arch discharged from his waist and into the air, splattering onto the burnt orange, shag rug.

Camille Thomas stood to her feet, wiped her mouth with the back of her hand, and scratched her ass.

"Fifty bucks," she spoke in a monotone voice.

"For what? You ain't doing shit."

In a defensive gesture, she folded her arms across her chest and slowly repeated, "Fifty bucks."

Camille reached for the partially crumpled Newport Menthol 100s from the aged end table. "I need some smokes," she huffed.

With a quick roll of the eyes and snap of the neck, "Lisha!" she called out as she turned her back to the stranger zipping up his tattered denim pants.

As if propelled by an explosive force, Jalisha hopped up from the bed and darted toward her bedroom door. She recognized the 'about to get your ass whipped' tone in her mother's voice. When she tried to speak, her voice wavered. "Yes, Ma'am."

"Get in here, girlie."

Jalisha flinched at Camille's order. She became more uncomfortable by the minute as her dismay grew. What now, she thought to herself.

Camille faced the stranger, tilted her head back, and peered at his face with disgust. "I said fifty bucks," she growled, her eyebrows raised into a perfect arch.

She amused him. "Woman, you crazy," he chuckled. "I want more than you wettin' my dick."

"Well that's all you gonna get," she snapped, rolling her eyes toward Jalisha.

Jalisha entered the living room, her head lowered, hands folded behind her back, and her face clouded with uneasiness. Nervously, she bit down on her bottom lip.

Camille reached into her skirt pocket and pulled out a twenty. She purposely lowered her voice to be mysterious. She knew how doing so kept her girls in line.

"Run to the store and get me a pack of smokes," Camille ordered as she balled up the twenty and tossed it at Jalisha, where it bounced off her chest and onto the floor. "Bring me my change back."

Anxious to escape from Camille's disturbing presence, Jalisha reached down, snatched up the twenty, and ran out the front door, leaving Corine hunched down in the corner behind the bedroom door with her face pressed against the crack and her eagle eye focused on Camille.

Camille smoothed her bangs with her fingertips. Her eyes squinted. "A'ight, niggah, I ain't gonna tell you no more. Give me my damn money and roll the fuck out," she demanded. She wrapped her chapped lips around the cigarette, while the tip turned a bright, fiery orange as she inhaled deeply.

"Yeah, I'll give you your money, but you will give me my monies' worth first."

She drew deeply on the cigarette and slowly blew a cloud into the stranger's face. "Niggah, I ain't giving you shit," she declared as she turned her back on the stranger.

With the swiftness of a sprinter, the stranger snatched Camille by the arm and yanked her toward him. "Look here, bitch. Don't be fuckin' with me," he snapped, showering Camille's face with his venom. "Now, you want fifty bucks and I wants me some pussy." His grip tightened. "You gonna give me what I pay for." His eyes were cold as ice. She shivered from the chill ravishing through her.

Fear whisked across her face. "A'ight, damn. Chill out, niggah," she whined.

Roughly, he thrust her away from him and straightened himself. The imprint of his hand throbbed down to her bone. "You want some pussy, it's gonna cost you twenty extra," she sniffed as she wiped her nose with the back of her hand.

His brows drew together in an angry frown.

"Okay, okay, damn. I'll give you what you want. However, let the record show this pussy ain't cheap. So next time you bring your cheap ass around here and you want a blow and some ass, make sure you bring enough money," she informed. She had pushed the envelope. The possibility of getting her ass whipped had mounted.

Camille turned her back toward him, bent over, and pressed her palms flat against the badly-in-need-of-paint wall.

He walked up on her and raised her skirt up to her head, resting it on her shoulders.

"Come on, niggah. I ain't got all damn day," she sighed.

He unzipped his pants and allowed them to fall down around his ankles. He bent at the knees and positioned himself so his waist would be level with her hind part. He stuck his index finger inside his ear and pulled out a glob of earwax. He then pulled her underwear to the side. A tart odor shot from her snatch up to his nose and throughout the apartment. He wrinkled up his nose, leaned his head back, poked out his chapped bottom lip, and inserted his index finger into her vagina.

"Finger fucks are extra, niggah!"

"Making sure you ain't got nuttin'. You don't smell so fresh."

He wiggled his finger in, out, and around her walls. Camille flinched. He pushed his finger deeper inside, purposely scrapping against her walls. For a hot second, Camille's feet left the floor.

He jumped back, smacked her on the ass, left his imprint, and snatched up his pants. "Bitch, you nasty! Naw, I don't want that shit and I ain't giving you fifty dollars!"

"Keep ya goddamn money and get the hell out. Don't bring your tired lil' dick 'round here no mo'."

He smacked her on the ass again as hard as he could.

"Ouch, bastard!" she cried.

"You need to stop selling tainted pussy!" he howled.

As he reached for the door, Camille picked up a porcelain vase, filled with a polyester floral arrangement of reds and blacks, and threw it. The vase crashed against the wall. It barely missed his head.

"Bitch, is you crazy?" His eyes grew large as he stomped toward Camille. "Is you crazy?" He raised his arm in the air and like an axe; he swung his fist down across her face. She tumbled to the floor like a freshly cut oak tree.

"Get out! Get out!" she hollered. "Before I call 5-0."

He grabbed her by the throat, lifted her up off the floor, and brought her eye level to him. "You need to be taught some manners." The back of his hand landed across her face. She crashed to the floor. He balled a clump of her hair within his fist and dragged her to the back of the apartment toward the bathroom.

Corine stood in her bedroom doorway, crying, "Mama! Mama!"

"Get back, Corey," Camille cried as she kicked, screamed, and pulled at the man's arm, trying to release his grip.

He dragged her into the bathroom and slammed the door. He picked her up, kicking legs and all, and dropped her into the tub. The impact of her body with the porcelain tub immediately calmed her. He reached for the Caress Shower Gel and emptied the bottle on her. Then, he turned on the shower and drew the shower curtain closed.

"Take your stank ass to the clinic," he snarled before making a hasty exit.

Corine stood sobbing in the doorway, "Mama?"

Camille whimpered as she tried to pull herself out of the tub.

"Mama? Are you okay, Mama?"

"Come here, baby, and help Mama," she whispered, reaching toward Corine.

Corine darted to Camille's side and quickly pulled back the shower curtain. She spun around at the slam of the front door.

"Lisha!" Corine cried. "Lisha, it's Mama!" She cried hysterically, her face flushed, resembling a child that was out in the cold too long.

Jalisha dropped the bag on the floor at the sound of Corine's cries and rushed to the bathroom.

"What's going on?"

"It's Mama! That man hurt her," Corine cried hysterically. "He put her in the tub and turned the water on her and then. . ."

"Help me up, Lisha," Camille whispered, reaching out for her.

"Oh Mama, look at you. You all bruised up," Jalisha said as she gently took Camille by the arm and helped her out of the tub.

"Mama will be okay, baby," Camille confirmed.

Camille grabbed hold of Jalisha and pulled herself up. Jalisha firmly planted her feet to the floor, trying to maintain her grip on Camille.

"Mama, you want me to call an ambulance?" Jalisha asked as she pulled a towel from the ceramic rack and wrapped it around Camille's shoulders. "You need to go to the hospital." Her voice was fragile and shaking.

"I'll be fine. Help me to my bed. I'm tired."

Camille tossed her arm around Jalisha's neck and leaned on her petite frame.

"Mama, I don't know why you keep doing what you're doing. It ain't safe."

Camille stopped abruptly and tightened her grip around Jalisha's neck. "Watch your mouth, girl. You eat and got clothes on your back, ain't cha?"

"Yes, Mama."

"If you think you can do better. . ." Camille sighed. "It's because of your sorry ass Daddy. If he paid some damn support, I wouldn't have to do this. Be happy you don't have to do it," Camille barked, her voice sounded tired.

"Mama, you bleedin'," Corine said, following on

their heels like a lost puppy dog, her eyes wide with innocence.

"Get a towel from the bathroom. . .and wet it," Jalisha ordered.

Corine darted to the bathroom and stared at the faucet. She looked confused. "Lisha, hot or cold water?"

"What? It doesn't matter, Corey!"

Corine turned on the faucet until the water was piping hot and the sink had filled. She turned off the faucet, grabbed an aged beach towel from beneath the sink, and tossed it into the hot water. She watched the beach towel absorb the piping hot water.

"Corey, what are you doing?" Jalisha asked in disgust. She had become irritated with Corine. She always felt Corine moved like an old woman to be so young. At times, she thought Corine border-lined retarded.

Corine pulled the hot towel from the sink. "Hssss!" She dropped the towel into the sink. "It's too hot!"

"Bring it!" Camille yelled.

Corine looked around the bathroom and eyed the toilet plunger. A light bulb went off. She grabbed the plunger, scooped the hot, wet towel from the sink, and carried it into Camille's bedroom, leaving tiny pools of water on the linoleum floor in the hallway.

"Here you go, Mama. This will make you feel better," Corine smiled as she dropped the hot, wet towel in Camille's lap. Camille was too numb to feel the scorching towel.

Corine sat on the bed, making note of every bruise and bump. "Mama?"

"What is it, Corey?" she sighed as she fell backward onto the bed and rested her eyes.

Jalisha removed the hot towel from her mother's bruised thighs and blotted the blood from her wound.

"I don't need to eat and I can wear Lisha's clothes..." Corine trailed off.

"Stop talking foolish," Camille snapped.

"I can get a job too, Mama," Jalisha offered.

"Doin' what?" Camille inquired.

"I dunno. . ."

"I can get a job too, Mama," Corine copied.

Camille opened one eye with a raised brow. "Y'all really don't want me doing that, do ya?"

Corine and Jalisha vigorously shook their heads no.

"I don't wanna do it either, but there ain't no job out there that is going to pay me what I make doin' what I do."

"Could you try to find one, Mama?" Corine asked.

Camille smiled at her concerned daughters. "Yeah, Mama will try to find one." And give up making all of this good money? Don't think so, she thought.

Corine and Camille's faces lit up like full moons.

# Chapter 2

The next evening.

"She said she wasn't gonna do that no more," Corine whispered, while Camille's headboard banged against her bedroom wall. "She lied to us."

Jalisha sat on the edge of the bed, quiet as a mouse.

"You hear me, Lish? I thought. . ."

"Shut up, Corey. How you gonna eat if she don't do it?"

"But she said she was gonna find another job."

"Well, I guess she couldn't find one."

"I think she like it," Corine pouted.

Jalisha looked at Corine and smirked. "What do you know?"

Corine grunted. "I know I have to use the bathroom."

"You have to hold it. You not suppose to leave the room when she has company."

"He ain't no company and I gotta pee, Lisha!" Corine jumped to her feet, grabbed her crotch, and crossed her legs. "I gotta pee!" She bounced up and down as if she had springs attached to her feet.

"A'ight, Corey. But you have to be real quiet."

"You go with me, Lish."

Jalisha took a deep sigh of irritation. "Come on and be quiet."

Corine and Jalisha tiptoed to the door and into the hallway. The headboard pounding against the wall grew louder. Camille's moans were deep and strong. The nasty tone of the stranger's voice stopped them in their tracks.

"Turn your ass ova!" he bellowed.

Camille panted for air like a worn out dog. "That's gonna cost you extra. But you need to use the Vaseline on the nightstand."

"I don't need no damn Vaseline," he barked.

"Look, niggah. Grease yo shit first," Camille snapped, and tooted her tail up in the air like a Pekingese in heat.

Corine and Jalisha glanced at each other and leaned forward to peek inside Camille's bedroom. They watched as the stranger greased the palm of his hand with Vaseline and then, like shaking a bottle, he briskly stroked his penis.

Next, he inserted two fat fingers into the jar, retrieved a small mound, and slapped it between Camille's dimpled buttocks.

The girls exchanged looks and turned up their noses.

"Damn, niggah, save some. I do have other tricks, ya' know?"

He packed the Vaseline in her rectum and slowly inserted his penis. Camille released a deep-throated groan at his entry.

As his thrusts grew harder and faster, Camille's groans grew deeper like a wolf howling at a full moon. It frightened Corine, but Jalisha wasn't moved at all.

Jalisha's attention diverted from Camille's romp to the stream of urine flowing down Corine's leg.

## *Chapter 3*

"Come on, Corey!" Jalisha exclaimed. "We gonna be late for school."

"I don't feel like going to school."

"You don't have a choice," Jalisha said, slipping into a pair of worn jeans. She looks at Corine inquisitively. "Why don't you want to go to school? You love school."

Lying in bed, Corine pouted and crossed her arms across her chest. "They say mean things."

Jalisha took a seat at the foot of the full-sized bed they shared. "Who is they and what are they saying?"

"The kids at school. They say things about Mama."

"Like what, Corey?"

"Like she nasty and she a whore; selling her body and stuff like that." Corine's nose tingled and tears formed around the ridges of her eyes. "Why they say such mean things, Lish?"

Jalisha stroked Corine's toes through the bedcovers.

"But what they say is true," Corine cried. "I don't want to live here no more."

"Hush, Corey. You don't know what you're saying. Where would you go?"

"To live with Daddy."

"Daddy?" Jalisha stood to her feet. "He don't wanna have nothin' to do with us," she scolded.

Catching herself, she lowered her voice. "You heard what Mama said."

Corine sat up in the bed. "How we know she's tellin' the truth? She already lied to us."

The sound of Camille stumbling out of bed startled the girls.

"Get your clothes on and come on," Jalisha ordered.

"I don't wanna. . ."

"We not going to school," Jalisha snapped in a huff.

"Where we going?"

"Y'all get out of here," Camille called out. "Y'all gonna be late," she mumbled. "I need some time to myself."

Camille felt her way down the dark hallway to answer the early morning knock at the door. With one eye plastered to the peephole, she asked, "Who is it?" Her voice was hoarse with frustration.

"I want some puss," came from the other side of the door.

"It's too early," she barked.

"I've got money," the voice pleaded with the magic word. Money.

Camille removed the chain and unlocked the door. It was time to get to work. She glanced over her shoulder as her daughters came down the narrow hallway.

"Get back in your room. I'll let you know when you can come out."

Knowing the routine all too well, the girls made a U-turn into their bedroom and closed the door.

"It's gonna cost you extra this damn early," Camille barked, swinging the door open.

"That ain't a problem."

Without brushing her teeth or taking a much-needed bath, Camille lifted her robe and pulled down her dingy underwear. She leaned on the arm of the sofa, stretched her legs apart, and raised her ass in the air.

The man without a name dropped his pants down around his ankles and leaned forward, pressing himself against her back and kissing her on the nape of her neck.

"No kissin'. Straight fucks only."

"No problem," he moaned, inserting himself into her dry wolf pussy.

Ten minutes later, the john was out the door and Camille had an extra seventy-five dollars in her pocket.

# Chapter 4

Now and Later wrappers and sunflower seed shells lined the corridors. The echo of laughter blared through Richardson Middle School.

"I thought you said we weren't coming here," Corine sulked.

"If we don't come to school, we get in trouble. Do you want that?"

"No."

"Okay then."

"What if they start talkin' 'bout Mama again?"

"Well. . .umm," Jalisha knelt down before her sister, "you don't allow anyone to talk about Mama. You hear me?"

"What do I do?"

"Go upside their heads. That's what you do."

"For real?" Corine's face lit up. "But I might get detention or suspended if I hit somebody."

Jalisha twisted her lips up in thought. "Yeah, I guess you're right." She stood upright. "If anyone picks with you or talks about Mama, you tell me and we'll get them together. Okay?"

Corine smiled at the thought of doing something, anything, together with her sister. She loved her sister more than she loved anyone.

"Good. Now get to class and I'll see you at lunch."

Corine threw herself against Jalisha and wrapped her arms around her. "I love you, Lisha," she whispered.

"I love you too, Corey."

Standing in the lunch line of the school cafeteria, Jalisha watched as the cafeteria lady plopped a glob of mashed potatoes onto her faded green plastic tray. She frowned up her face and moved down to the next cafeteria lady who tossed a dry piece of meat favoring meatloaf onto her tray.

"What's that?" she asked.

"What does it look like?" the woman snarled, ruffling her thin, hairline mustache.

"It looks like something you feed a dog," Jalisha snapped.

"Move down!" the woman barked. "Or get out of line!"

Jalisha moved down the line and watched as the third cafeteria lady spooned mixed salad onto her tray.

"Thank you," Jalisha frowned, looking disgusted at the mound of crap atop her tray. Jalisha reached for a carton of chocolate milk and handed the cashier her lunch ticket. "Why can't we eat what the teachers eat?" she asked the cashier.

The cashier forced a smile and said, "Because you ain't no teacher. Move on!"

Jalisha rolled her eyes and exited the line. She stood beside the silver waist high freezer and looked inside. She reached in and pulled out a Neapolitan ice cream sandwich.

"Lisha, Lisha!" Corey ran up to her, almost running into her tray.

"What Corey? Dang, you gonna make me drop my tray. What is it?"

"They were talkin' 'bout Mama again. This time he said his brother's dick had green stuff coming out of it and it was all because Mama was nasty."

Jalisha felt herself fuming. Tears streamed down Corine's face. "Who is he, Corey?"

"Timothy Booth," she accused as she pointed in his direction.

Timothy sat at the white bench-style table and joshed with the other children, while throwing food across the table.

"Cut it out, Timothy!" the little girl exclaimed. "I'm going to report you!"

"So! I don't care who you tell," he teased.

Jalisha approached Timothy from behind and tapped him on his shoulder. "Is your name Timothy?"

"Yeah," he said, turning to face Jalisha. His eyes darted from Corine to Jalisha. "What's it to you?"

"I don't appreciate you talkin' 'bout my mother the way you been doin'," Jalisha said with much attitude, her neck twisting in a full circle.

"I ain't say nuffin' 'bout your mother," he lied.

"Yes you did!" Corine interjected. "You said your brother. . ."

Jalisha elbowed Corine. "Hush, Corey."

"I ain't say nuffin' that ain't true," Timothy confessed.

"Whether it is true or not, don't talk about our mother no more. You understand me, lil' boy?"

"Oooh, I'm shakin'," he teased. "Oooh, I'm real scared."

Irritated by his taunts, Jalisha took a deep inhale. WHAM!

Jalisha crashed her tray over Timothy's head. Mashed potatoes, dried meatloaf and brown, wilted salad was the crown that adorned the King of Bratstown's head.

The children seated at the table erupted in laughter.

"I'm gonna tell," he cried, running out of the cafeteria.

"Come on, Corey," Jalisha instructed. "We're going home."

Corey stuck her tongue out at the children seated at the table and proudly followed behind her big sister.

# *Chapter 5*

Before Jalisha's key entered the lock to the apartment, Camille's laughter wafted into the hallway. She hesitated and thought twice about interrupting another one of Camille's client meetings. She shook it off and inserted her key, unlocked the door and entered.

"What're y'all doin' here?" Camille asked, with her legs draped across another man Jalisha didn't recognize.

"They let us out early," Jalisha said, spitting out the best lie she could contrive under the circumstances.

"Who's that, Mama?" Corine asked.

Jalisha nudged Corine with her elbow. Corine had forgotten rule number three of Camille's list.

Rule #1: Jalisha and Corine are not to open the door if they hear three knocks in a row, because, most likely, it's one of Camille's johns.

Rule #2: Before Camille opens the door, Jalisha and Corine are to rush to their room, close the door, and not come out until Camille instructs them to do so.

Rule #3: Never, ever ask any questions. Period.

Camille's piercing glare put the fear into Corine. "I'm sorry, Mama."

"Go to your room," Camille ordered.

Corine lowered her head.

"Come on, Corey," Jalisha said, disgusted with having to always go to their room. "I'm sick of this,"

Jalisha mumbled.

The cigarette dangled from Camille's bottom lip. "What did you say?"

Jalisha increased her pace to her bedroom. "Nothing."

"I don't know what has gotten into Miss Grown Ass, but I intend to put a stop to it right now," Camille said to her company.

Camille rose to her feet as the girls' bedroom door closed. "I'll be back," she said as she marched down the narrow hall, ready for battle.

Camille pushed open the bedroom door with such force, the knob hit the wall, adding a baseball-sized hole to the already gloomy decor. She approached Jalisha, her jaw muscles tightened.

SLAP! SLAP!

Camille's hand nearly knocked Jalisha's head off her shoulders.

Jalisha gasped as tears quickly streamed down her cheeks.

"You little bitch! You think you grown?"

"No," Jalisha whimpered.

With a thread of warning in her voice, Camille slowly asked, "No, what?"

Jalisha's tears choked her. "No, Ma'am."

"I suggest you get your attitude in check, Missy. Humph, don't see you paying one bill in this house or puttin' any food on the table or paying the damn rent. I don't see your ass out here hustling. . ." she trailed off, losing herself in thought. "You think you're grown, huh?"

"No," Jalisha responded.

Camille shifted her weight, placed one hand on her hip, and stared at Jalisha.

Trembling like a leaf, Jalisha responded, "No, Ma'am," to Camille's glare.

"Uh huh, since you don't like what I'm doing, maybe you can do better. What you think, huh?"

Jalisha's stomach knotted and she stiffened from what she feared Camille had in mind.

Corey interjected her plea for her sister. "She didn't mean it, Mama."

Camille turned to Corine. "Go outside. I want to talk to your sister."

"But, Mama. . ."

"Now, Corey!" Camilla ordered sternly.

Corine slowly walked from the bedroom to the front door. "When can I come back in, Mama?"

"When I tell you to," Camille yelled, slamming the bedroom door.

Jalisha moved toward the bed.

"So, you think you can do better than me?" Camille asked, walking toward Jalisha.

Jalisha shook her head no.

"Answer me," Camille snapped. "You ain't a damn mute."

Jalisha replied in a small-frightened voice. "No, Ma'am."

Camille grunted and dropped her cigarette butt to the floor, putting it out with her foot. "Pick that up and put it in the trash can," she scowled between clinched teeth.

Jalisha hesitated. She began to shake. A mixture of fear and anger knotted inside her.

"Lisha, I will smack you silly."

As Jalisha bent down to pick up the cigarette butt, Camille smacked her on the behind as hard as she could.

"Don't you talk back to me. Do you understand me? I work my ass off so you and your sister can have food in your stomachs and clothes on your selfish backs. Your damn trifling ass Daddy ain't doing shit for you. But since you feel I ain't providing for you, then you need to get your lil' hot ass to work." Camille leaned back and sized up Jalisha. "Yeah, it's time you earned your keep."

Camille stormed out of the room.

Jalisha fell backward onto the bed and took a sigh of relief. Jalisha closed her eyes and tried to relax.

"Lisha, get out here," Camille yelled from the living room. "Hurry up!"

"Yes, Ma'am," she whispered as she sluggishly pulled herself off the bed. She wiped her face with the back of her hand and slowly walked toward the living room. Her head was lowered as her hands dangled by her side.

"Lisha, this is Mr. Ben, one of my regulars. He's agreed to be your first customer."

Lisha raised her head in shock, her mouth wide open and eyes wide with concern. "No, Mama. Please."

Mr. Ben's face brightened at the thought of breaking in a virgin.

"Ain't she pretty," Mr. Ben admired. "Nice lips too. They look soft as cotton."

Camille wrapped her arms around Jalisha and pulled her into a phony embrace. "Uh huh, the apple doesn't fall too far from the tree." Camille smiled proudly.

"Freshly picked off the apple tree – never bruised," Mr. Ben smiled and exposed a mouth filled with disgusting rotten teeth.

Lisha cringed and wept uncontrollably.

"You ain't got time for tears, girl."

"Mama, I don't want to do this."

"Girl, he gonna pay you good money."

"But, Mama, I. . .I. . . ."

"Lisha, you are gonna help me out. You will handle all of the blowjobs and I'll handle everything else."

Mr. Ben unzipped his pants, reached in, pulled out his penis, and stroked it.

Camille shoved Jalisha toward Mr. Ben.

"Come on, baby. Mr. Ben won't hurt you," he said. "You'll like it, I promise."

"We ain't got all day, Lisha!"

Jalisha's face was soaked with her salty tears.

Mr. Ben used his thumb and wiped away her tears. He leaned in and kissed her soft cheek.

"No. No kissin'. You know that!" Camille snapped. "You don't need to put your damn hands on her."

"I'm trying to make her feel comfortable, that's all."

"She don't need to feel comfortable when she's gotta job to do."

Jalisha tried to hold back her urine, she was so afraid.

Camille walked up behind Jalisha and whispered in her ear. "If you don't drop to your knees and do your job, I'm gonna skin your ass alive. Do you hear me?"

Jalisha nodded her acknowledgement and got down

on her knees. Reluctantly, she scooted closer to Mr. Ben's crotch. She looked up at him. The look in her eyes was heartbreaking, but he didn't give a damn. He wanted a blow and didn't care who performed it. However, he thought it to be sad Camille would pimp her own daughter.

"Camille, since she's so young, it should be half price, right?"

"Hell naw, niggah. A blowjob is a blowjob. Regular price."

"She swallows?"

"Sure, she swallows." She looked down at her daughter. "Don't you, baby?"

Jalisha didn't say a word. She didn't move. She was frozen.

Mr. Ben inched himself closer toward Jalisha's face. He palmed the back of her head and brought her face into him, where he inserted his softness into the warmth of her delicate, infantile mouth.

Jalisha closed her eyes and pretended she was in another place and time.

With the assistance of Mr. Ben, Jalisha brought him to full climax.

Then, she threw up on his penis.

# *Chapter 6*

Six years later, in the dark, damp alley behind the housing project, four floors beneath her bedroom window, sixteen-year-old Jalisha posed in front of Robert, her regular trick.

"Hey, when can I get more?" Robert inquired as he pulled at her waist.

"More what?"

"More of you."

"Rob, you ask me all the time," she giggled. "I only do blowjobs, you know that. Have been for six years. Ain't nothin' gonna change."

"So you saying you still a virgin?"

"Chit chat will cost you extra," she smiled.

"Now you sound like your damn mama."

"The apple doesn't fall far from the tree," she mumbled Camille's exact words, as she thought back to her first trick, Mr. Ben.

"When you ready to put a price tag on that ass, I wanna be the first to pop that sweet cherry." He smiled, licking his lips.

She propped her hand on her hips. "This alley shit is for the birds."

"What's wrong with your place?"

"Camille has that on lockdown."

"Damn, she put you out to trick and don't give you a place," he chuckled.

"Yeah, well. . .anyway, fifty bucks."

Robert reached into his pocket and pulled out two twenties and a ten. "It was worth it. You need to teach Camille how to give head before you end up taking all of her customers."

"I don't plan on doing this forever, Rob. I want to do something with my life. That's why I don't do fucks, because I ain't tryin' to get pregnant or catch shit."

"Well, I wish you luck, baby girl. Once you start trickin', and livin' in the projects too, it's hard to stop or get out."

"Humph, not me. Maybe for Camille 'cause she likes doin' this shit. Me, I don't like it."

"Then why you doin' it?"

"Because we need the money."

Robert chuckled. "I seriously doubt that. Not at what Camille charges to sell her ass."

"You know how much she charges?"

"Don't you?"

"No. She never told us and we never asked."

"Fifty for blowjobs, seventy-five for anal and a straight fuck, and one-fifty for all-nighters."

"Damn. . ."

"Yeah, and no disrespect, but Camille's ass is like seven-eleven – open twenty-four hours, seven days a week. So you know she's raking up."

"She's always tellin' us she never has no money."

"Well, you do the math."

"Yo, Jalisha. You tryin' to make some money?" came from across the street.

Jalisha looked in the direction of the question. "I'll check you later, Rob."

She trotted across the street and conversed with the tall, sun-drenched man with a defined muscular build.

"What you tryin' to do?" he asked.

"You know I only suck dick. You want something different, see Camille."

"Damn, you bitches got the market cornered."

"Whatever. You want a blow or what?"

He nodded and grabbed her by the arm.

"Where we going?" she asked. "The alley is across the street."

"Baby, I don't do  alley shit. We go to my crib. Is that okay with you?"

She hesitated and thought for a minute. She knew him from seeing him around but she didn't know his name. She looked him up and down and figured it would be all right to go with him since everyone in the 'hood knew who he was, including Camille—he was a dedicated regular of hers.

"Yeah, a'ight. Let's go," she agreed.

Inside, she dropped her purse on the end table by the door and stood in the middle of the floor. "Okay, let's make this quick, shall we?"

"I'm not paying for a quickie, babe."

"I only do blow jobs," she reiterated for the hundredth time.

"Maybe it's time you changed your policy."

"Look. . ."

"All I want is a little cuddling and passion."

"It's gonna cost you extra…the cuddling, that is. I don't do passion."

"I can't hold you?"

"Hold me? Niggah, you trippin'. Look, why don't you look up Camille?"

"I don't want Camille. I want you."

"A'ight," she said, taking a step closer. "If you want me, then you play by my rules. Cool?"

"And they are?"

"No passion and no fuckin'."

"Let me make sure I got this straight. I can kiss you. . ."

"Naw, you can't kiss me."

"Okay. . .I can hold you, caress you, suck on your tits, and even stick my finger in your puss?"

"Uh huh, but all that shit gonna cost you extra."

He took a step backward and sized her up. "It will be worth it," he smiled. For a moment, she felt special. "What're you drinking?"

"I don't drink."

"You sure? Soda? Milk?"

"That's real funny. What's your name?"

"Derek."

"Oh. . ."

"Get comfortable, Jalisha," he offered, pouring himself a snifter of Crown Royal.

Jalisha took a seat. She wasn't used to the nice treatment and being spoken to so nicely by her tricks. This was definitely a first and she liked it.

Derek took a seat beside her and crossed his leg. He leaned in to her and held the glass of Crown Royal close to her face. The rim softly touched her bottom lip. "Are you sure you don't want a drink?"

"I'm sure, thank you."

"It's smooth," he smiled. "Like your skin."

Jalisha smiled and adjusted herself on the sofa. Something about Derek was making her uncomfortable.

Derek wasn't her usual trick. He was Camille's. He also didn't live in the Lincoln Heights Housing Projects. Derek lived three blocks from the projects, on Division Avenue. Word has it his parents died and left him the house. He has a job, a car, no baby's mama, and no girlfriend.

Jalisha took a sip from the snifter and twisted up her face.

Derek smiled at her innocence and placed the snifter on the glass-topped coffee table. He took her hand in his. "Jalisha, why are you selling yourself short?"

"I'm not. I charge for my services."

"That's not what I mean," he chuckled.

"Well, what do you mean?"

"Why are you turning tricks?"

"Because we need the money."

"Do you like turning tricks?"

"Naw, I don't like it. But. . ."

"There are no buts, Lisha. If you don't like doing it, then don't do it."

Jalisha turned her head away from Derek.

He used his index finger and turned her face toward him. "You are too beautiful to be doing this." He gazed into her eyes. The intensity of his glare drove her crazy. He leaned in and grazed her bottom lip.

A chill shot through her body. She shivered.

"Are you cold?" He wrapped his arm around her shoulder.

She was unable to speak. She felt something she'd never felt before, passion.

He pulled her into him and embraced her lips. His tongue was the key to open the lock on her lips.

Camille's 'no kissing' rule ran rampant through her mind, but she ignored it. She relaxed herself under his arm and reciprocated her first serious kiss.

He rested his hand in her crotch and caressed her.

She grabbed his hand, pulled away from him, and stood to her feet. "No fuckin'," she barked.

"You said I could touch you."

"Not if it's gonna lead to you trying to fuck me. Don't touch me that way."

"Okay, okay." He raised his hands in the air. "You're still a virgin?"

"Uh huh," she grunted.

"You might like it," he smiled.

"Nope," she replied with a twist of her neck. "I don't do that." She propped her hands on her hips. "And I see you can't follow instructions, so I better go." She proceeded toward the door.

"No!" He jumped to his feet. "I mean . . . don't go, Jalisha. I'm sorry. I'll do what you want."

Jalisha faced the door with her hand tightly affixed to the doorknob.

"Come on, Lisha," he pleaded.

Jalisha inhaled deeply and relaxed her tensed shoulders.

"I'm sorry, all right?"

She turned and looked at him inquisitively.

"You have my word. Whatever you want to do, we'll do."

"For real?"

"Yes."

"Suppose I don't want to give you a blow?"

"Then don't," he sighed as he shifted his weight from left to right. "You don't have to do anything you don't want to do."

She turned her lips up in thought and nodded her head. "I'll hang around," she smiled.

"Good," Derek smiled. He picked up his snifter and took a sip, his eyes focused on her.

"Can I have some?" She pointed at the bottle of Crown Royal.

Derek extended his glass. She took the glass and raised it to her lips.

"Sip it," he instructed. "Don't take a mouthful."

She nodded and took a sip. She leaned her head back and allowed it to flow down her throat as it burned her chest.

"You like it?"

She smiled and took another sip.

Derek took a seat on the worn, soft blue velveteen sofa. "You're very beautiful, Jalisha. You smell good, too. I can smell you all the way over here."

Jalisha bashfully lowered her head.

"Come sit down." He patted the vacant space beside him.

Without hesitation, Jalisha filled the vacancy. She took another sip and emptied the snifter, then extended it for a refill.

He obliged her with Crown Royal to the rim.

She took a few more big sips. She liked the way the brandy made her feel. The only alcohol she knew of was Schlitz Malt Liquor Bull, also known as a forty.

Derek leaned in to her and sniffed her neck. "You sure smell sweet, Lisha," he whispered.

Derek talked into her neck and sent chills all over her, causing the hairs on her arms to stand at attention. He stroked his nose against her neck. "Hmmm," he moaned. His hand found its way beneath her dress and softly stroked the top of her thigh. "Your skin is so soft."

Jalisha quickly panted with pleasure.

He stroked his tongue in a circular motion around her neck, while his hand pried her thighs apart.

She shook her head no.

He cupped his lips over hers, while his finger eased beneath her underwear, playing with her pubic hair.

Jalisha enjoyed his touch and ignored her cardinal rule. She inched down and slid her hips to the edge of the sofa.

Derek inserted his finger into her snatch, where he poked and prodded her walls.

"Derek. . .it feels so good," she cooed as she moved her hips in an upward motion, making slight slapping sounds against the palm of his hand. "Oooh, yes. . ."

"I want to feel you," he faintly whispered in her ear.

"No," she flatly said.

"The head, let me put the head in."

"I don't do penetration."

"I'll pay extra." His pants were dry and rough. "Come on, Lish. Please. I've wanted you for the longest." He felt around inside her for the tiny bump on the ceiling of her vagina as the palm of his hand rubbed against her swollen lump.

Jalisha knew this was wrong, 'cause it felt too good to her. "You got a rubber?"

"Naw, I ain't got no rubber."

"I don't know, Derek."

"Lish, I ain't gonna come inside you."

"I don't wanna get pregnant."

"You won't. I'll pull out before I come."

Jalisha thought for a moment. "You sure you gonna pull out? Don't be comin' all up in me, Derek!"

"Yeah, I told you I would," he promised.

Jalisha, lying down on the sofa, pulled her underwear down around her ankles.

Derek climbed on top of her.

"You better pull out, Derek. I mean it," she warned.

"Damn, baby. I said I was, didn't I?"

With her legs pulled back against her chest and her underwear dangling from her ankle, Derek inserted his key into her ignition and took a ride around her virgin hood.

Jalisha groaned and flinched at the pain from his thrusts.

"Hmmm," he groaned deeply. "Damn, you got some good pussy."

"Slow down, Derek. That hurts."

He increased his speed. "Oh shit!"

"What?"

"Oh shit!"

"What, Derek?"

"I'm about to come."

"Take it out!"

"Damn, this shit is good as fuck!"

"Take it out!" she yelled as she attempted to push his six-foot-one, muscular frame off her.

"Arghhhhhhh," he groaned from deep within. His face distorted as his pounding intensified.

Tears streamed down her face as the fire between her legs increased.

Derek wilted on top of her from exhaustion. "Virgin pussy is the best," he smiled, kissing her on the cheek.

Jalisha lowered her legs and encircled him. She felt his semen nest inside her. "You promised, Derek." She stared through him. "You promised."

"I'm sorry, baby. I. . .I. . .couldn't control it."

"I don't wanna get pregnant," she wept.

Reality bit Derek in his ass as he has realized his possible fate of fatherhood, not to mention the legal ramifications of a twenty-three-year-old fornicating with a sixteen-year-old girl. He slid down to the floor.

"When was the last time you had your period?" he inquired.

"Last week. Why?"

"I don't know, but I heard if you have sex right before your period, you won't get pregnant."

"Really?" Her face brightened from the ounce of hope.

"Yeah. . ." he responded confused as hell. In all actuality, he didn't know what he was talking about.

"What about after your period?"

"I don't know. . ." he trailed off into deep thought.

"What if I'm pregnant, Derek?"

"You ain't pregnant, a'ight? Chill on that shit."

"But. . ."

"But nothin', Lish." He stood to his feet in irritation. "Look, how much do I owe you?"

Jalisha looked at him in amazement.

He extended his wallet toward her. "How much?"

"You don't have enough to pay me for stealing my virginity."

"You gave it to me," he snarled. "Get the fuck out!"

"Derek. . ."

"Naw, ain't no Derek. I want you out of my crib."

Jalisha rose to her feet. She had experienced the popping of her cherry, and Derek's semen mixed with her cherry juice streamed down her inner thighs.

"Get out!" he barked.

She looked at him, gathered her belongings, as well as her composure, and slowly walked toward the door. "I don't know why, Derek, but I thought you were different."

Derek opened the door, looked outside, and then at Jalisha. "You still here?"

# *Chapter 7*

Jalisha stood inside the tiny foyer of the apartment. She dropped her purse to the floor and, in a daze, walked to the bathroom. She closed the door behind her and locked it. She looked into the mirror and no longer recognized Jalisha. Who she saw was the creation of Camille. She broke down into tears. She throbbed between her legs. She drew herself a warm bath and soaked for hours. She held her breath and immerged herself under water. She thought about releasing her breath and allowing the water to fill her lungs. Then Corine's face flashed before her and she couldn't leave her sister behind to fend for herself against Camille.

Corine stooped outside the bathroom door and peeped through the keyhole. She watched Jalisha emerge under water. She covered the keyhole with her lips and whispered so Camille wouldn't hear her. She was supposed to be in the bed. "Lish? You okay?"

"I'm fine."

"You've been in there for a long time."

"I know."

"Can I come in?"

"I'll be out in a minute. I'll meet you in the room, okay?"

"Why you trying to drown yourself?"

"Corey, leave me alone," Jalisha snapped.

Jalisha pulled herself from the chilled bath water

and stood naked. Water dripped on the black and white tiled floor as she stared at the red tinted bath water. She pulled the stopper and watched as remnants of her virginity swirled down the drain and headed toward the Potomac River. She reached for Camille's bathrobe hanging on the back of the door, which was off limits, and slowly slipped into it as if her body ached. She pulled a clean towel from the wall unit positioned above the toilet and winced as she wiped between her legs.

The telephone rang as she opened the bathroom door. After the fourth ring, Camille answered the phone. Camille did not allow the girls to answer the phone.

"Jalisha! Telephone, girl, and don't be tying up my line," Camille yelled from the living room.

Jalisha took her sweet time, knowing it was bugging the hell out of Camille. She shot Camille a look of disgust and snatched the phone from her claws.

"Jalisha, have you lost your mind?" Camille snapped. "What the hell is your problem?"

Jalisha ignored Camille's typical ranting and raving and placed the phone against her ear. "Hello," she whispered into the receiver.

"Lisha?"

"Who's this?" she asked, annoyed as she plopped down on the sofa.

"This is Derek."

Calmness overcame her, and she put a deaf ear to Camille's cursing her like a rugged sailor.

"Lisha, you there?"

"I'm here."

Derek took a deep sigh. She could sense he was having a hard time trying to find his words. "I'm sorry."

She didn't respond. His words wrapped around her and soothed the throbbing between her legs. No one, other than Corine, had ever spoken those two words to her.

"Jalisha, I'm sorry. I was wrong. I got carried away. . .hell, there's no excuse for the way I acted. Believe it or not, my parents raised me better than that."

"Okay," she whispered. She tried to hold back the tears, but she was unsuccessful.

"No, it's not okay. I was out of line. Can you find it in your heart to forgive me?"

"Yeah, I guess."

"I'd like to see you again, if it's okay."

"Umm. . .I dunno," she mumbled, her eyes followed Camille's every move.

He cleared his throat. "Well, if not, I understand."

In the kitchen, Camille rummaged through the refrigerator. She hadn't been to the grocery store in weeks, so she saw nothing that tickled her fancy.

"You need to get off my damn phone. You don't pay the fuckin' bill!" Camille yelled from the kitchen.

"I gotta go."

"Tonight. Let's grab something to eat. Where do you want to go?"

Without thinking, she pulled Applebee's off the top of her head.

"Great! I'll pick you up at. . ."

"Can you come by at eight? Camille will be out tonight."

"Okay. I'll see you then."

# *Chapter 8*

Jalisha hung up the phone and tossed it on the sofa beside her. She looked around and mumbled, "This place is a sty." She pulled herself up from the sofa.

Meanwhile, Camille was still in the kitchen where she attempted to prepare dinner —freezer-burned hot dogs with no buns. "Who was that?" Camille asked as she stood in the kitchen scratching her crotch.

Jalisha lowered her head and refused to answer. After all, she felt it was none of her damn business if she was talking on the phone.

"I asked you a question, and are you wearing my robe?"

"Nobody, Ma'am."

"Take it off!"

Jalisha looked confused.

"Take off my robe," Camille snarled.

"But. . ."

SMACK!

Camille smacked the mess out of Jalisha and sent her flying against the wall. "Take my shit off, now! Because you suck a little dick here and there, don't mean you are me!"

With her hand pressed against her cheek, Jalisha removed the robe and stood in the middle of the living room. She was naked and trembling like a leaf.

Camille examined Jalisha. Her eyes roamed up and

down her body where they stopped below her waist. Camille took a step closer, leaned in, sniffed, and took a step backward. She looked into Jalisha's eyes. Jalisha refused to make eye contact.

"Your cherry been popped yet?"

"Ma'am?"

Camille took a step closer. Warmth exuded from her body.

"Don't play with me, girl," she drawled slowly between clinched teeth.

Camille could always tell when Jalisha was lying because her eyes blinked uncontrollably, and Jalisha's eyes were on a roll.

"I. . ."

Camille turned her back to Jalisha. "You know ain't nothing worse than a liar, Lisha. So, don't lie to me."

"I'm still. . ."

POW!

The blow against Jalisha's head cut her lie short.

"You liar! Get out of my damn face!" Camille blared as she stomped toward her room.

Corine poked her head out from her bedroom with eyes as big as golf balls.

"Get back in your room!" she yelled at Corine. "I'm going out, and Lisha, your fast ass better not leave this house!" she instructed as her door slammed shut.

Camille slipped on her dress, slid into her shoes, grabbed her sweater, and headed for the front door. She entered the living room and glared down at Jalisha as she pulled herself to her feet. "Don't leave this house. No tricks, no nothing. You got me?"

"Yes, Ma'am," she sobbed.

# Apple Tree

Camille stormed out the door without so much as a lick of water or a dollop of soap.

# Chapter 9

Corine sat on the terracotta and cream bedspread and watched as Jalisha lined her lips with coal black eyeliner. "Why do you want your lips to stand out like that?" Corine asked with her head slightly tilted.

Jalisha rolled her eyes at her annoying younger sister as she colored Princess Purple by Posner lipstick within the black lines, giving her full lips a deep purple hue. "Girl, you don't know what you're talking about."

"I know when something doesn't look right," Corine jived.

"You have no clue," Jalisha snapped. "But then again, you're only a child."

Corine rounded her shoulders and tooted up her head. "I am not a child. I am thirteen years old!"

It always bothered Corine to no end. Jalisha, who was only three years older than she, would call her a child when Jalisha was a mere child herself, trying to act like a grown woman.

Corine sat and watched as Jalisha puckered her lips in the mirror, turning her head from side to side, making sure there were no flaws on her cafe au lait complexion. She touched up her mascara and gently outlined her hazel eyes. She took a step back from the chest of drawers, adorned with white lace doilies, and admired her five-foot-five voluptuous frame. At sixteen, she could easily pass for a sultry twenty. Satisfied with the image before her, she reached for her dollar store fragrance and sprayed around her neck, between her cleavage, and finished with a squirt between her thighs, for just in case.

"That's nasty," Corine smirked, her nose twisted like she smelled a skunk or something rotten. "Why are you putting stuff down there?"

"See? You are a child. If you were a woman like me," Jalisha turned her back to the mirror, looked over her shoulder, and admired her round posterior, "you would know why you should squirt a little fragrance down there."

Corine folded her arms across her chest and poked out her lips. "I wonder what Mama would think if I told her you were spraying perfume between your legs."

"Mama won't say nothin' 'cause you ain't gonna tell her," Jalisha grimaced at Corine.

"Humph, think I won't?"

"If you tell Mama, then I will tell everyone you are thirteen and you still don't have your period."

Corine huffed, puffed, and stood to her feet. "You make me sick!"

A smile of triumph crept across Jalisha's face. "That's what I thought."

"I'ma still tell Mama," Corine mumbled under her breath, while looking down at her hot pink canvas tennis shoes. They were the perfect match for her hot pink and lime green striped tank top and hot pink panties. She doesn't have a stitch of trousers on.

When inside the house, Corine never wore pants. They irritated her crotch and caused her panties to ride up between her buttocks. Since her mother told her it wasn't nice for young girls to pick their underwear from their behinds, she decided not to wear pants, at least not around the house.

Corine fell back onto the bed and stared aimlessly at the spinning ceiling fan. She felt dizzy and wasn't sure if it was from her constant stare of the ceiling fan or the tremendous amount of perfume Jalisha had sprayed on herself and between her legs.

Jalisha slipped on her royal blue and fuchsia polka-dotted sundress and peered down at Corine. "Corey, zip me up, please."

Corine took a deep sigh and then pulled herself upright to face the lower part of Jalisha's back. "Where are you going?"

Jalisha inhaled as Corine zipped up her dress, catching a piece of skin in the zipper. "Ouch!" Jalisha flinched and jerked around to face Corine. "I should slap the piss out of you!"

"I'm sorry! It was an accident."

Jalisha turned up her lips and glared at Corine as she smoothed her dress over her size twenty-four hips. "Derek is taking me to Applebee's tonight."

"That's it?"

"Yep."

"Then why are you getting dressed up to go there?"

"Because I can," Jalisha barked. "Will you please put some pants on? Derek will be here soon and he doesn't need to see your flat-as-a-pancake tail walking 'round here with no clothes on."

Jalisha primped in the mirror once more before she fetched her matching handbag from the thirty-six-inch-wide closet, where all of her thrift store hand-me-downs protruded.

"Does Mama know you're going out tonight?" Corine asked, stomping on her sister's heels.

"No, she doesn't. I'll be home long before Mama gets back."

Jalisha entered the living room, tossed her handbag on the sofa, and aimed for the mirror hanging in the tiny foyer of the Lincoln Heights Housing Projects apartment.

"Does Mama know you are wearing her dress?"

Jalisha jerked around to face Corine. She grabbed Corine's arm and dug her fingernails deep into her delicate, petite arm. "Listen, you better keep your mouth shut, you hear me?"

Corine's eyes grew so large, they looked like they were about to pop out of her head. "That hurts, Lish!" she cried as tears streamed over her high cheekbones, forming a river down her cinnamon complexion.

At the sound of the knock at the door, Jalisha released her arm and pushed her toward the sofa, causing her to lose her footing and fall back onto the sofa.

"That's Derek. Either put some pants on or get in the room," Jalisha snapped. She turned to face the mirror and smoothed her hair with her fingertips. Corine didn't budge. "Get!" she yelled, causing Corine to jump to her feet and flee for the bedroom they both shared.

"I'ma tell Mama!" Corine cried, slamming the bedroom door behind her.

Jalisha rolled her eyes at the door, took a deep

breath, and responded to the constant knock. "Hey, Derek, come on in," she smiled, stepping to the side for him to enter. "Would you care for a soda or something?"

"Naw, I'm good," he said, looking around the tiny apartment. "You alone?"

"No. My lil' sister's in the bedroom."

"Oh," he said, planting a kiss on her lips.

"Umm, you ready to go?" Jalisha asked.

"Where's Camille?"

"She's out."

Derek closed the door and pressed Jalisha against the wall. "You are so beautiful."

"Thanks," she smiled. "Derek, my sister is. . ."

"I know," he said, looking down the corridor toward the bedrooms. "She can't hear us." He pulled her dress up around her waist. "Spread your legs a little."

Mesmerized by him, she did as instructed.

Derek knelt down before her and brushed his face against her thighs.

"What are you doing?" she giggled.

"Giving you what you deserve," he responded, pulling her panties down around her ankles. "Step out of these," he instructed as his gaze met hers. "When you're with me, panties aren't required."

Derek nuzzled his face inside her warmth, explored her flesh, and stroked her bud. Jalisha braced herself against the wall, ready to accept the pleasure she had heard so much about. She felt she was ready.. Within seconds, she experienced her first orgasm. Her knees felt weak, almost buckling beneath her.

# AppleTree

Derek wiped his mouth on her thigh, took her by the hand, and they headed for Applebee's.

# *Chapter 10*

Inside his white '79 Mazda RX-7, Derek's hand nestled between Jalisha's thighs. Jalisha tried to maintain her composure as he played with her. This was all new to her.

As the RX-7 turned the corner, Jalisha spotted Camille climbing the steps and entering the apartment. Unconsciously, Jalisha tightened her thighs on Derek's hand.

"Whoa, babe. You gonna cut off my circulation."

"Sorry. Can we go to your place instead?" she asked, not wanting to confront Camille, especially when she had violated the 'don't leave the house' rule. She thought about Corine and hoped she wouldn't get the brunt of what she had coming to her for disobeying Camille.

A smile crept across Derek's lips. "Sure, we can go to my house. What you tryin' to do?"

Jalisha slid down in the seat and partially opened her legs. "What you wanna do?" she teased.

Derek flipped a U-turn and sped off to his place. Once they pulled up in front of his place, he removed his hand from her crotch and inserted his finger in his mouth, slowly pulling it out. "You taste good."

"You are silly," she giggled and let herself out of the car.

"Silly for you, boo," he cooed.

Once inside, before Derek could close the door, his pants were around his ankles and his member was at attention.

Out of habit, Jalisha immediately dropped to her knees and brought him to full climax.

The next morning, Jalisha woke up to Derek's body intertwined with hers. She had stayed out all night and dreaded the consequences she would have to endure from Camille.

There's no need to rush, she thought. Camille is going to have my ass no matter what.

"Good morning, baby." Derek smiled and gave her a kiss on the cheek.

"Good morning."

"How are you feeling?" he asked.

"I'm feeling fine. Why?"

"How do you feel about staying the night with me?"

"I don't feel anything."

"Did you enjoy it?"

"Yes. I've never had anyone to do me like that."

"So what does this mean?" he asked.

"This means Camille is going to whip my ass, that's what it means."

Derek chuckled. "Yeah, well, I guess your mother will be pissed you stayed out all night, especially with you being only sixteen."

"No kidding."

He detected a hint of fear in her response. "Don't worry. I won't let anything happen to you," he said as he slid beneath the sheet and crawled between her legs.

"Ohhhhh!" she cooed as Derek's sucking lips grabbed hold of her swollen bud. "Awww. . .Oh my," she groaned as she balled the bed sheets into the palm of her hands. "Yessssssssssssssssssssss!" she screamed as she raised her hips for Derek to suck harder.

Jalisha's body wilted as her legs dropped around Derek's shoulder.

"Mothafuckaaaaaaaaaaaaaaaaaaaaaaaaaaaaaaaaaaa!" she howled from deep within.

"Damn, that was a hard one," Derek said as he wiped her from his lips with the back of his hand.

Jalisha turned on her side and cuddled the pillow.

"Baby, you hungry?"

She nodded her head and closed her eyes.

"Okay, I'll fix you breakfast."

"Okay," she whispered, then fell off to sleep.

# *Chapter 11*

The door closed behind Jalisha at four o'clock in the afternoon.

Camille sat on the sofa puffing on a cigarette, with her leg propped over the arm of the sofa. "Where in the fuck have you been?" Camille yelled.

"Lisha!" Corine cried as she ran up to her sister. "I was worried about you."

"I'm okay, Corey."

"Where the fuck have you been, Lisha?"

"Out," Jalisha snapped.

Jalisha was feeling her oats and besides, she was going to get the beat down anyway, so why shouldn't she tell Camille what is on her mind?

Camille leaned back. "Who the fuck. . .are you getting a fuckin' attitude?"

"I'm tired of you riding my back, Camille."

"Camille? Camille? Oh, I see. Your ass is grown now, huh?"

"No, I'm tired and don't feel like no mess, that's all."

"Corey go to your room!" Camille ordered. "We need to have a talkie talk."

Corine looked at Camille and then at Jalisha.

"Go, Corey. I'll be in there in a minute. Okay?"

Corine nodded her head and slowly walked to her bedroom.

"A'ight, what's up, Camille?"

"Lisha, don't you disrespect me in my fuckin' house!"

"Sorry."

"Yeah, you sorry all right. You a sorry ass bitch, that's what you are," Camille snapped, retrieving a cigarette from the pack and placing it on her bottom lip where it dangled. "Who in the fuck do you think you are? You ain't grown, Jalisha. You are only sixteen. I told your ass not to leave this house and you did it anyway." Camille tossed the cigarette pack on the end table and pulled her lighter from her pocket. She lit her cigarette, took a drag, and slowly exhaled. "You were out all night. You must've been fuckin'!"

"I wasn't fuckin' nobody."

Camille's eyes grew large. "I beg your pardon?"

"You heard me." The words expelled from Jalisha, slow and with venom.

Camille slowly pulled herself up from the sofa and walked over to Jalisha. They stood toe to toe. She turned up her nose. "You smell like a whore."

"I smell like you!"

Camille knocked Jalisha onto the sofa and pounced on top of her. "You wanna be grown!" she yelled, her punches hard as rocks.

"Get off of me!"

Camille forced her hand up Jalisha's dress and felt around for her missing underwear. "Open your legs!"

"No!"

"Open them!"

"No!"

With force, Camille pried open Jalisha's legs and

rammed four fingers inside her. "Damnit!" she yelled, inserting her fifth finger. "You whore!"

"Stop it! You're hurting me!"

With additional force, Camille rammed her fist inside Jalisha. A sharp howl escaped from Jalisha.

Corine darted from her bedroom toward the brawl. "Get off of her!" Corine yelled, pulling at Camille. "Leave her alone!"

"Go back, Corey!" Jalisha cried. "Get back."

"Get off of her! Stop it!" Corine cried.

"Corey, if you don't get off of me, I'ma whip your ass too!" Camille exclaimed and pushed Corine with force.

Corine fell against the china closet and landed on her behind. She jumped to her feet and ran to her room. She hollered and screamed to the top of her lungs.

"Camille, please! Stop it! It won't happen again," Jalisha cried.

Camille struck Jalisha in the stomach. "You're going to end up pregnant, you dumb ass cunt!"

"Please stop it!"

Corine shot from her bedroom, hollering and screaming. "Stop it! Stop it!" She came up behind Camille holding a ceramic figurine Jalisha gave her last year for her birthday.

"No, Corey!" Jalisha yelled.

As Camille turned to face Corine, the figurine struck her temple. Her grip on Jalisha loosened and she fell over onto the floor. Her body flopped around like a fish out of water.

Corine dropped the figurine and ran to Jalisha.

Jalisha consoled Corine and looked down at Camille.
"Did I kill her?"

"I don't know."

"I didn't mean to. I wanted her to stop hurting you, Lisha," she cried.

"Everything will be okay."

"What are we going to do?"

Jalisha gathered herself and reached for the phone. She dialed Derek's number. "Derek, it's Lisha."

"Hey you. . ."

"Derek!" she screamed.

"What's wrong?"

"Can you come over?"

"Uhh, yeah," he hesitated. "I guess. What's wrong, Lish?"

"Come over now, please," she begged.

"On my way."

# *Chapter 12*

Corine stood over Camille's body and wept. "Lisha, am I going to jail?"

"No, you aren't going to jail."

"Then what's gonna happen to me?"

"Nothin' is gonna happen to you. Derek is going to take care of everything."

"How you know you can trust him?"

How could she trust Derek? She didn't really know him. "I don't know. . ." she trailed off. Suppose he reports this to the police, she thought to herself. "I shouldn't have called him, but I didn't know what else to do," she confided to Corine.

Corine slumped to the floor. "Are they going to split us apart?"

"Who is they, Corey?"

"The welfare people."

"No, they won't split us, 'cause we won't tell them. Now, go put some pants on."

Corine pulled herself up. "Does this mean  we can do whatever we want to do?" She looked down at Camille's lifeless body. "We don't have her telling us what to do no more." A slight smile formed on her face. "I really didn't like her no way."

"Corey, cut it out. Don't talk like that. She's our mother, regardless."

"Should we say a prayer or something?" Corine tilted her head to the side.

"For what? You want to pray over a sinner?"

"What's a sinner?"

Jalisha pointed at Camille.

There was a constant knock at the door. "Lisha, it's me. Open up."

"Derek!" Jalisha exclaimed. She swung the door open and fell into his arms.

Derek looked over Jalisha's shoulder and saw Camille lying on the floor in a fetal position. He broke their embrace and held her at arm's length from him. "What happened, Lish?" He looked into her eyes for answers.

"It got out of control," she said, looking at Corine. "Put some pants on!" she snapped.

Derek glanced at Corine as she hauled ass to the bedroom.

"Is she dead?" Derek asked, walking toward Camille's body.

"I think so."

"You didn't call the ambulance?"

"No!"

"But why. . ."

"I don't want Corey to get in trouble."

"Corey did this?"

Jalisha nodded her head. "She didn't mean to do it."

"I think you better tell me what happened, Lish."

"Well," she sniffed, "when I came home this afternoon, from being out with you, Camille was pissed. She asked me where I'd been and when I wouldn't tell her, she got even more pissed and she started beating on me. She knocked me on the sofa and started sticking her fist in my...in my..." She broke down in a convulsed cry.

"It's okay, baby. I'm not here to judge you. I want to get a handle on what happened so I will know how to proceed."

"Corey was trying to get Camille off of me, but Camille wouldn't stop. So, Corey went into the bedroom and got that porcelain doll..." She trailed off, pointing to the shattered statue.

"Okay, I got the picture," he said, resting his hands on his hips.

"Derek, what are we going to do?"

"We?"

"Yes. I thought you and I...well..."

Derek raised his hands in front of him. "Hold up, Jalisha. I don't want nothing to do with this mess."

"But I thought after last night, you were...you know."

"Last night was last night. This is something totally different. Do you know what this is? This is murder. A niggah could get life for this shit!"

Jalisha instantly became enraged. "Fine! You don't have to help me. I see you ain't no different than the other mothafuckas out there. I should've charged your punk ass!"

"A'ight, you ain't gotta go there. You know I care about you."

"Fuck you, niggah. You don't give a shit about me. All you care about is the pussy. You got it, you were the first, so go tell all of your friends and get the fuck outta my house."

Derek readjusted his weight and exhaled. He closed his eyes and grounded his back teeth. He punched his fist into thin air. "Okay. I'ma help you."

"What you gonna do?"

"We are gonna dump the body."

"Dump it where?"

"I don't know."

"How we gonna get her out the building without people seeing us?"

"Hmmm," he pondered. "That's a good question." Derek began pacing the floor. "Y'all got anything to drink?"

"Soda and milk."

"That's it?" Derek asked, hoping for something stronger.

"Yeah."

Derek faced Jalisha. "I got it!" he exclaimed in excitement.

"What?"

"Is there a basement in this building?"

"Yeah, why?"

"Is there a storage room or something?"

"Yeah, next to the laundry room. Why?"

Derek hovered over Camille. "You are going to have to help me. She looks heavy."

"Okay, what we gonna do?"

"We are going to take her down to the storage room and put her there. Someone will find her and think she was murdered by someone else."

"You think it will work?"

"Yeah, it'll work. Someone will think  she had a trick gonna bad or something."

Jalisha didn't feel any remorse for what had happened to her mother. "Corey, stay in your room."

Corine ran from the back. "Why do I have to stay in the room?"

"Because I said so, that's why."

She moped back to her room. "I'm getting mighty sick of that room," she mumbled.

Derek reached down and grabbed Camille by her ankles. "You get her arms," he instructed.

Jalisha grabbed Camille by both wrists and they hoisted her in the air and stretched her like a Mambo pole.

"What do we do now?" Jalisha asked.

"We take her ass down in the storage room and be done with it."

"Corey, come here," Derek called.

"No, I don't want her to see this."

"Lisha, she's the one who cracked her upside the head. We need her help."

Corine skipped from the back. "Oh, I can come out now," she sung.

"I need you to make sure the coast is clear in the hall," Derek ordered.

"How low can you go? How low can you go?" Corine sang, as she mamboed beneath Camille.

"Cut it out, Corey!" Jalisha snapped. "This ain't no damn game."

Corine took a deep sigh, rolled her eyes, and sucked her teeth. "I can't never have no fun," she whined, making her way to the door. With her hand affixed to the doorknob, she turned toward Derek. "What you want me to do again?"

"Open the damn door and let me know if it's clear," he barked.

Corine rolled her eyes, twisted her neck, and opened the door. She looked left, right, and left again. She took a step backward and opened the door wider. "Coast is clear."

Derek and Jalisha crept down the narrow corridor and down the steps toward the basement. Camille's body swung left to right and bounced off the railing.

Corine crept up behind Jalisha and whispered, "Are we gonna get in trouble?"

Startled by Corine, Jalisha released Camille's wrists and Derek tumbled down the stairs. "Damnit, Corey! Get back inside!" Jalisha exclaimed. "Derek, you okay?"

"Shit! Yeah, I'm okay." He pulled himself to his feet and grabbed Camille's ankles. "Grab her and let's get her downstairs."

Inside the storage room, Jalisha released Camille and Derek dragged her lifeless body on the cold, damp concrete and propped her in the corner.

"I need something to throw over her," he said.

"Why?"

"So nobody will see her, that's why."

Jalisha grabbed the old, moth-eaten pea-green blanket she spotted in an unlocked bin and tossed it at Derek, where it landed at his feet. When Derek reached down to pick up the blanket, a mouse shot from out of nowhere and scurried between Camille's legs and into her hideaway. Jalisha screeched and took off up the steps, while Derek tossed the blanket over Camille's head and ran for the hills.

# *Chapter 13*

"What are we going to do now?" Corine asked as she twiddled the ruffled trim on her blouse between her thumb and index finger.

Jalisha sat quietly, not knowing how to contemplate her next move. She'd never been in this position before. What was she going to do? She knew making money would be easy. Camille taught her that much. However, she also knew she didn't like what Camille had become and she didn't want to end up the same way — used, abused, filled with infections, and tossed to the side.

"Well, I guess we call Daddy." Jalisha nestled her chin between her knees.

"But he doesn't want us. Remember what Mama said?" Corine whined.

"Well where else we gonna go?"

"We can stay here. Can't we?"

"Not for long," Jalisha said, lowering her head to rest between her knees. "They will be looking for us soon."

"Who is they?"

"Child Protective Services. Once they find out about Mama, they are going to split us up and we'll probably never see each other again," Jalisha cried.

"Jalisha, I don't wanna be away from you," Corine cried.

"No. I won't let that happen."

## *Chapter 14*

Thoughts of Camille haunted her dreams — the cold stare of her eyes and her limp body. Jalisha tossed and turned restlessly. She balled covers up around her neck and left Corine to shiver from the cold drafts floating about the apartment. Camille had made tons of money selling her ass and still the heat was off.

Jalisha rose up in the bed and, through the darkness, focused her eyes, looking around the small bedroom. The first thing she knew she had to do was leave the apartment. She knew she and Corine couldn't stay there. Where would they go? She wondered if Camille had stashed money somewhere, seeing as though she didn't go anywhere to spend it.

She tossed her legs over the side of the bed, rested the bottoms of her feet on the cold, linoleum floor, and wrapped her arms around herself in an attempt to stay warm. As the chill from the cool drafts surrounded her, she pulled herself from the bed and tiptoed to the closet, careful not to wake Corine. She reached in her closet and pulled out a white, moth-eaten wool sweater Camille had given her several Christmases ago. Camille was famous for outfitting the girls at the Salvation Army or Value Village thrift stores.

A loud pound at the front door aroused her from her deep thoughts and Corine from her slumber.

"Who is that, Lisha?"

"Now how do I know who it is?" she snapped. "Stay put," she ordered Corine, while she slipped out of the bedroom and walked slowly toward the front door.

She pondered over the idea of the police coming to haul Corine off to jail. She stopped in her tracks. The knocking continued, more persistent. She reached for the door and softly asked, "Who is it?" with her eye plastered to the peephole.

"Camille there?"

Jalisha hesitated. Her stomach curdled like two-week-old sour milk. "Naw, she ain't here."

"Who's taking care of her business while she's gone?"

Jalisha contemplated the stranger's question and slowly opened the door. "That depends on what you want. . ."

"The usual."

"It's kinda late. Camille don't usually take customers this late."

"Yeah, well I'm an exception," he barked. "Now you gonna take care of me or what?"

Jalisha opened the door wider for him to enter.

The stranger looked her up and down and smiled. He flashed a hole where there once was a tooth and several black crevices inside his mouth.

Jalisha led the man to Camille's bedroom. She felt like she was about to work the best little whorehouse in DC. She could see Corine peeping through the crack of their bedroom door as fear cast over her face.

"It's okay, Corey," she whispered. She hoped to have softened her sister's concerns.

Inside Camille's bedroom, the stranger closed the door behind them and turned Jalisha to face him.

"How old are you?"

"Old enough to take care of business while Camille's away," she said. She instantly transformed into a professional.

"All right, since you old enough, I want my usual."

"And that is?"

"Turn around, pull down your draws, and I'll show you."

"I don't do anal."

"I don't do anal either."

Jalisha nodded her head and did as she was told. She felt in total control.

"Bend over," he ordered. "Lay your hands flat on the bed."

Thoughts ran amuck through her mind as the swift sound of leather cracked through the air. She whipped around and faced the stranger.

"Don't look at me," he ordered. "Keep your hands flat and if you flinch, it will only get worse."

Tears began streaming down Jalisha's soft, delicate cheeks. Fear of what laid before her caused her body to tremble.

WHACK! WHACK! WHACK!

Jalisha's mouth flew open and expelled gut wrenching cries as the leather crashed against her buttocks.

WHACK! WHACK! WHACK!

Jalisha's cries were hard and unforced, like a wild animal.

WHACK! WHACK! WHACK!

The stranger's erection bulged through his trousers.
WHACK! WHACK! WHACK!

"Please stop!" Jalisha cried, her ass red as a rose. "Please stop!"

WHACK! WHACK! WHACK!

The stranger dropped his pants down around his ankles and moved in closer to Jalisha's inflamed rear end.

"Don't move," he ordered sternly.

Jalisha sobbed and prayed it would be over soon. She couldn't imagine how Camille suffered through such torture. Why wasn't Camille more selective? Where did she find these perverts?

The stranger released his erection and used his fingers to spread apart her reddened cheeks. The sight of the welts across her cheeks had really turned him on.

"You're clean?" he asked.

"What?"

"Is your pussy clean? You seem real young, so your pussy probably clean."

SMACK! SMACK! SMACK!

The palm of his hand landed across her butt cheek as he inserted his hardness between her lips. He penetrated her dryness and pulled back the skin of his penis.

"Damn! You too damn dry," he spewed.

He removed himself, bent down, lowered his face between her thighs, gathered saliva, and spat his moisture between her legs where it landed in her bush.

SMACK! SMACK! SMACK!

He inserted himself and meshed his saliva within her crevice. He stroked her fierce and hard.

SMACK! SMACK! SMACK!

Jalisha's cries were of a wounded animal badly wanting to lick its wounds.

SMACK! SMACK! SMACK!

She pushed herself into him. She was beginning to enjoy the pain preceding the pleasure.

"Yes!" she yelled, giving into his madness. "Fuck me!" she yelled. "Don't stop! Yessss!"

"You want me to smack that ass again?"

"Yes!"

SMACK! SMACK! SMACK!

Jalisha pumped herself into his abdomen. She wanted him to pound her harder. She balled up the sheets in the palm of her hand and demanded he stroke her harder.

With each command, the stranger pounded against her crimson-welted flesh.

"Aww shit, motherfucker! You gonna fuck me harder or get the fuck out!" she heard herself say.

The stranger removed himself, retrieved the leather belt, and gazed down upon Jalisha's inflamed buttocks.

Corine could not believe her ears. Tears slowly found their way down her cheeks while confusion jumbled her mind.

Corine closed her eyes tight. Jalisha's yells reminded her too much of Camille.

"Stop it! Stop!" she whispered. Her body trembled. She wrapped herself in a cocoon with her comforter.

In her short life, she saw too much and witnessed too many painful scenes.

She bit down on her lip until it throbbed rapidly, like the beat of her heart. Corine couldn't take it anymore. She sung her favorite song to calm her. A song Camille used to sing to her when she was a little girl. "You are my sunshine," she sung through tears, her voice wavered. "My only sunshine."

"You want to be fucked harder, huh?"

Jalisha turned to face the stranger. Tearstains formed dry riverbeds down her cheeks. She stood quietly.

"Lie on your back, spread your legs, and I'll give you what you want," he said.

Jalisha laid flat on her back and closed her eyes.

"Put your hands on the bottoms of your feet."

His request confused her. This was all new to her, although she was enjoying every minute of it.

"Don't move," he snarled. "Pull your ankles real close together."

He tied the leather belt around her ankles and wrists. He made sure she wasn't able to move, and then he removed his left shoe.

WHACK! WHACK! WHACK!

Jalisha howled at the heel of his shoe connecting against her vaginal lips.

WHACK! WHACK! WHACK!

Jalisha's cries quickly turned to that of an infant.

WHACK! WHACK! WHACK!

The stranger's erection hardened at the sight of Jalisha's redness. He was about to explode. He lowered himself to the edge of the bed and rammed himself inside her. Again, peeling back foreskin.

"Girl, what's with your dry ass?"

Again, he removed himself, but this time, he lowered his face into her mound and roughly sucked at her lips where he pulled and tugged with his teeth.

Jalisha hissed at the feel-good pain inflicted upon her swollen lips.

He continued tugging and pulling at her clitoris, sharpening his teeth.

"Not so hard!"

He ignored her cry.

"Not so hard!" she cried.

He released her clitoris and roughly inserted himself between her thighs. He stroked her continuously for one hour until she was extremely raw and sore.

"When are you going to come?" she asked through tears.

"I don't come in sluts. I just fuck them."

The stranger laid his pipe until the sun came up.

Jalisha's legs were exhausted and cramped. She laid there lifeless and numb. He pulled his erect tool from between her throbbing legs, pulled up his pants, and tossed a one-hundred-dollar bill toward her. It landed on her chest.

He untied her ankles and wrists. He watched as her limbs fell lifeless to the bed.

And with a springy bounce, he was gone.

# Chapter 15

When the front door slammed, Corine crept into Camille's bedroom. Jalisha was curled in a fetal position.

Corine leaned lightly toward Jalisha and tilted her face toward hers. "You want me to call 9-1-1?"

Jalisha shook her head violently.

"You want me to get a wet rag?"

"Yes," Jalisha whispered.

Corine darted for the bathroom and returned with a cool, damp washcloth. She cradled Jalisha in her arms and tended to her welts, but refused to wipe between her legs. This is too much for a sixteen-year-old girl to go through, she thought to herself.

To Corine's dismay, Jalisha wasn't a girl anymore. She was now a woman who had to do whatever it was she needed to do to keep her and her sister together.

Jalisha curled up beneath the sheets and rested. Corine crawled in behind her, wrapped her arms around the one she admired the most, and nestled her face in the crevice of Jalisha's neck.

"I love you, Lisha."

"I love you too, Corey." Jalisha placed her hand on Corine's arm. "We'll be fine."

I'm not going to let her do this all by herself, Corine thought. I'll pull my weight, too.

# *Chapter 16*

Two weeks later, the humidity and dampness sped Camille's body to decomposition. Her remains had succumbed to bacteria and smelled of an indescribable odor, which wafted throughout the building and caused quite a stir among the building's tenants. Her body, which was feasted on by rodents and insects, had decayed and turned green.

It was assumed Camille was murdered at the hands of a disgruntled customer. Simply, she was a whore who resided in the projects. One less whore they had to worry over.

# *Chapter 17*

Corine gazed down at Jalisha as she slept peacefully. She bent down and laced up her black leather, thigh-high stiletto boots. Her now thirteen-year-old, perky, just-graduated-to-training-bra, teardrop-shaped breast beamed through the knit halter-top as her thick bush peeked between her young thighs. She reached into the nightstand drawer and pulled out a strip of condoms from Jalisha's stash. As she reached for the doorknob, she looked over her shoulder and smiled at her sister. Lisha, you will be so proud of me, she thought.

Corine stepped into the cool night air and made her way eight blocks to the corner of East Capitol Street and Division Avenue. She never ventured too far from home when she turned her tricks. At two o'clock in the morning, traffic was light. She didn't think she would do much business at this time of night, but she couldn't sneak out earlier 'cause Jalisha insisted she complete her school assignments.

Since Jalisha dropped out of school to earn money for them, she was determined Corine finished school. Little did she know her educated baby sister was following in her whorish footsteps. They never had to do homework before. Camille could've cared less if they passed or failed. All she cared about was her fifty bucks she charged for a trick.

Corine annoyingly tugged at her skirt to keep out the early morning breeze.

A red sedan approached the curb, and the passenger window slowly rolled down.

"Hey, Sweet Mama," the snaggle-toothed saber called out. "Let me see what you're carrying, Mama. Bend over for me."

Corine sucked her teeth, rolled her eyes, and turned her back. She bent over and allowed the mini skirt to rise above her young cheeks.

"Whoowee," he squealed. "How much to taste that?"

"Fifty bucks," she said, mimicking Camille's famous saying. Truth was she didn't have a clue what to charge for her tricks.

He let out a deep sigh and said, "That's a lot for some puss. Are you a virgin?"

"If you want me to be."

"How old are you, sweetheart?"

"Old enough," she retorted angrily. "Look, cut the chitchat. You wanna do business or what?"

He leaned over to the passenger side and opened the door. "Get in," he said, salivating over her innocence.

"Naw, I don't get in strange cars. If you wanna do business, meet me in the alley around the corner."

He closed the door and drove down East Capitol Street. He made a right turn on 50th Street then an immediate right into the alley behind Ames Street.

Corine was standing at the other end of the alley, motioning for him to drive toward her.

He rolled down his window and Corine leaned into the car.

"Don't waste my time, niggah. You got fifty bucks or not?"

"Now what kinda language is that to come from such a pretty lil' girl?"

Corine took a deep sigh, squared her shoulders, turned on her heels, and walked away.

"Where ya going, honey?" He slowly followed behind her as she walked down the alley toward 50th Street. "Hey, lil' mama, I got the money."

She stopped in her tracks and turned to face the glaring headlights. She placed her hand on her hips and yelled, "Hurry up. I ain't got all night, niggah." The more she turned tricks, the more she heard herself sounding like Camille.

"Get in the car. It's cold out there," he offered. "I got the heat on."

He was right. It was cold as hell and her teenage ass felt like a block of ice. Corine rushed toward the car.

He opened the door for her and she hopped inside. The heat was blasting, and she was beginning to melt.

"What you want?" she asked, facing him.

"I want some virgin pussy," he smiled, flashing a mouth full of rotted teeth.

Corine cringed. She knew he wasn't a cop with such a nasty looking mouth. She was thankful she did not kiss her tricks.

"Let's get in the backseat," he suggested.

"What for?"

"Baby girl, I can't get my stroke on in the front seat."

Reluctantly, Corine opened the door.

"Oh no, baby girl, crawl over the seat. Let that pretty ass smile for me."

She rolled her eyes and started to crawl over the seat. As her abdomen straddled the front seat, she felt a finger insert into her pie. "Finger fucks are extra, niggah."

"Look-a-here, I ain't gonna be too many more niggahs."

"Finger fucks ain't free."

"I'm trying to see if you a virgin or not, and you ain't no virgin."

"I never said I was."

"Yes you did, you lying lil' bitch!" He splattered her with foul saliva.

He could stand an Altoid, she thought to herself as she held her breath and her lips tightly closed. She knew if she inhaled his breath through her mouth, she would throw up.

Corine quickly slipped into the backseat. She was frightened. She'd never been in the position of having to defend herself. She didn't know what to do. Calling out for Jalisha wasn't an option. Jalisha was a good half-mile away and fast asleep.

"It's not that serious," she said with a forced smile. "I'll let you have a free finger fuck this time," she whimpered. She took deep breaths, trying to slow the rapid beating of her heart. "Uhh, what's your name?"

The man smiled and replied, "I'm your daddy

tonight." He reached over the backseat and stroked her tender thighs. "You are a pretty thing, you are."

"Thank you," she stuttered. His touch felt clammy and frightened her to no end.

"Um hum, spread your legs for me," he gently ordered. He made a conscious effort not to yell. He didn't want to scare her.

Corine slightly parted her legs.

"A lil' wider, honey."

She closed her eyes and opened her legs as wide as they would open in the back seat of a car.

"Now, umm," he moaned, "put your legs up on the seat."

Afraid of what would happen if she didn't comply, she threw her legs across the front seat.

"Um hum, that's real good. Now, slide down and raise your hips."

"Why?" she whimpered.

"It's going to be all right. Just do what I tell you to do." This time, there was no sign of a smile on his face. His face was twisted and halfway looked abnormal.

Corine raised her hips so her cheeks were touching the cool leather seat.

"Daddy" scooted to the middle of the front seat and positioned himself before her. His head leaned into her youth. He inhaled deeply and stroked her clit with his tongue.

Corine flinched. She'd never experienced oral sex before. The stroke of his tongue against her clit sent an electric charge throughout her.

He wrapped his arms around her legs and clamped

down. He looked at her and asked, "Have you been a good little girl?"

His question confused her. "Huh?"

"Have you been a good little girl?"

Corine looked into his deep, midnight eyes. Fear and uncertainty aroused within her.

"That's good." He stroked her once more. He looked up at her with a wicked, satanic grin. "Have you heard of the Bunny Man?"

Corine shook her head. Tears welled in her eyes. "What's the Bunny Man?" she sobbed.

# Chapter 18

Is it fact or fiction?

The legend of the Bunny Man dates back thirty years.

A man dressed as a bunny haunted the residential neighborhoods around the Washington, DC metropolitan area. His travels led him to secluded locations told of a figure clad in a white bunny suit and armed with an axe, threatening children.

By the 1980s, the Bunny Man had become an even more sinister figure with several gruesome murders under his belt. Although he was reported as far south as Culpepper, Virginia, his main haunt was the area surrounding a railroad overpass near Fairfax Station, Virginia, and the now infamous Bunny Man Bridge.

Parents used this tale as a way of coaxing their children in the house when the streetlights came on.

"Child, you better get in here before the Bunny Man get you!"

It always worked.

# *Chapter 19*

His eyes squinted and his left brow rose into an arch. "I'm the Bunny Man," he responded, his voice grated harshly.

Corine tried to wiggle free, but his strength was ten times hers. "Please let me go!" she cried. "I won't tell anyone. I promise!"

"Shut up!" he yelled. "Do you want people to hear you?"

She vigorously shook her head and calmed down. "Please don't hurt me."

"I won't hurt you. I am going to save you." He leaned in between her legs and took her clit inside his mouth. His sucking soothed her. She was enjoying it, until his sucks became more forceful and hard.

"Ouch!" she exclaimed. "That hurts," she cried.

He ignored her cry, bit down harder, and severed her clitoris.

Corine cried so hard her voice faded as hot tears streamed down her cheeks.

He looked deranged, her severed flesh dangling between his teeth. He faced the dashboard and placed his hands in the ten and two o'clock positions on the steering wheel. With his right hand, he turned the ignition. Then he glanced at Corine through the fogged rearview mirror and grunted, "Quiet!"

Corine attempted to stifle her cry, but the pain was more than she could bear.

He shifted the gear into drive and sped off down the alley, coming to an abrupt halt on 50th Street. "Get out," he growled. "Get out." His voice was distant and withdrawn.

Corine felt weak and lightheaded. She slowly opened the rear passenger door and slithered into the alley, favoring a slippery snake.

The car skidded off.

She shielded her eyes as rocks and debris flew into her face and temporarily blinded her. The stench of the burning tires filled her throat and caused her to gag. Corine rolled over onto her back and called out, "Jalisha. Somebody please help me." Her cries continued until she realized each backyard housed a loud, obnoxious dog. She gathered her composure and attempted to stand to her feet. She was feeling weaker by the minute. She took eight steps and fell to the ground, flat on her face. She raised her head and looked both ways before dragging herself across Ames Street and up 50th Street toward Lincoln Heights.

The streets were unusually calm at three in the morning. No kids roamed the streets and no trace of drug deals gone bad.

When she reached her apartment building, her palms, knees, and thighs were scraped raw. Her energy to pull herself up four flights of steps had depleted. She decided to rest until morning.

The next morning, Jalisha's cry woke Lincoln Heights. "Oh my God! Corine!" Jalisha tugged at her sister. "Corine, what happened? Wake up, Corine! She ain't done nothing to nobody!"

Corine lay peacefully, hunched on the steps, soaked in a pool of red, and cradled in Jalisha's arms.

# *Chapter 20*

Jalisha wept as she stood in the city-run cemetery before the headstone that read:

*Corine J. Thomas*
*Born March 12, 1988*
*Died January 22, 2003*

There was no service, no mourners, and no family. Just Jalisha. Camille is buried in the same cemetery, but she didn't know exactly where. Camille didn't have a headstone, but a marker that read, "Jane Doe." Jalisha felt she had let her baby sister down and was determined to provide her with a headstone. It was the least she could do.

"I miss you so much, Corey. Things aren't the same without you. There's no more laughter and smiles. I'm going to move on though. Gotta find me a new place to stay. I found a wad of cash Camille had stashed under her mattress, at least a couple thousand," she hesitated. "I won't move too far. I'll try to stay close, although I don't know where to go. Oh, I called Daddy and Camille was right. He don't care about us. I told him about you and he acted like he didn't even care. How can you not care your own child is dead? He said you and Camille deserved what happened to you, but he's wrong. You didn't deserve it, Corey. The motherfucker who did this to you was sick. You didn't do anything wrong, and I don't want you to think you did. Well, I've gotta go now. I'll try to come back this weekend soon as I get settled in my new place, wherever it may be." Jalisha knelt down on the ground, leaned in, and kissed the headstone. She closed her eyes and recited the Lord's Prayer, what little bit she knew.

"I love you, Corey. Tell God I said hello."

She took in a deep breath, raised her face toward the sky, and allowed the sun to dry her tears.

# *Chapter 21*

Jalisha wrapped herself in the deep purple velveteen throw and nestled in the corner of the second-hand, floral pattern sofa. For the umpteenth time, she buried herself in her favorite read, *The Coldest Winter Ever*. She loved the novel because she saw so much of herself in Winter, the main character. At times, she felt as though Sistah Souljah had written the novel especially for her.

She also loved the writings of Maya Angelou. After she saw *Poetic Justice*, she memorized *Phenomenal Woman* and recited it to herself daily. She'd become an avid reader, for it was the only way she could escape the tawdry life chosen for her.

After chapter ten, she tossed the book to the other end of the sofa and took a long needed stretch. It wouldn't be long before she had to get ready for work.

It's been seven years and Jalisha hadn't been back to visit Corine's gravesite. She hoped Corine didn't hate her, but she couldn't bring herself to re-visit a place she knew would be her home soon, if she weren't careful.

After Corine's death, she vowed to change her life. Nevertheless, with no high school diploma, not even McDonald's would hire her. For a hot minute, she'd thought about running scams, instead of selling her ass to make a living. At least, she wouldn't continue to degrade herself on a daily basis. She tried the Pigeon

Drop, but taking advantage of the elderly didn't sit right with her, especially people who had done nothing to her. *I may be a whore, but I do have values,* she constantly thought.

Jalisha was forced to move from Lincoln Heights. Business was scarce. Customers wouldn't come within two feet of her. They labeled her the Lady of Death. Since she wasn't making as much money as she had been before Corine's death, she rented an apartment on 14th and P Streets. It was more affordable and around the corner from her workstation. It wasn't much, but it was home. Like Camille, she refused to pay good money for furniture. So, most of her Saturdays were spent in pawnshops, thrift stores, and yard sales.

Her apartment was quite quaint, with eggshell colored walls. She absolutely hated hardwood floors because it was cold to her feet. Therefore, she covered the floors with warm, chestnut-colored carpeting she found in the alley behind her apartment building. Since her profession was cold and lonely, it was important her surroundings were warm and cozy. Odd pieces of artwork she had picked up from the Salvation Army covered her walls. Her coffee table was adorned with *Shape, Parenting,* and *National Geographic* magazines she removed from the community clinic during her monthly visits. On the floor, beside her sofa, sat a magazine rack packed with *The Washington Post, New York Times* and *The Afro-American* newspapers. She was determined not to be the typical whore. She wanted to be a well-rounded and learned individual.

After her weekly visits to the thrift store, she stopped in at the public library and checked out every black history book her arms could hold. She loved learning; she couldn't get enough of it. She didn't plan to trick all of her life. She was still young, so she was determined to learn all her brain could absorb. Things will change for the better, she meditated daily.

She refused to have anything to do with a pimp. If she were the one selling her ass, then she would be the one keeping all of the tax-free profits. She and only she would set the price of her ass. The infamous 'fifty bucks' was at the top of her list. However, with the economy the way it was, she had 'sales' from time to time. It was getting hard to get a decent trick though. The Metropolitan Police heavily monitored the 'strip' and arrested anyone who attempted to solicit the services of a prostitute, even though many of DC's finest were regulars. Charging them a discounted rate kept her out of jail and on the street.

Jalisha pulled herself from the sofa and walked toward the kitchen. A nice cup of herbal tea would hit the spot, she thought. Before she reached the kitchen's threshold, she looked to her right and stared at the mirror image. Tears started to form around the edges of her eyes. She looked so old and worn. She was denied her youth and thrown headfirst into adulthood. For this, she could never bring herself to forgive Camille. As much as she tried, the deep burning hatred she harbored for her mother was an eternal flame. If she could not forget, then she could not forgive.

She wiped her eyes and entered the kitchen. She turned on the faucet, filled up the reddish orange teakettle, placed it on the stove, and ignited the gas flame beneath the kettle.

She reached for the Philly blunt she had rolled earlier, filled with seeds and stems. She held it between her pursed lips, leaned down toward the yellow-tipped, blue flame, and inhaled deeply. The sizzling sound of her hair cooking caused her to jerk upright, drop the burning cannabis, rush to the sink, turn on the faucet, and immerse her head. She reached for the dishcloth to wrap her wet tresses. She threw her head back and took a step backward. The pain was excruciating.

"Oooh, shit!" she yelled, lifting her leg and flinging her foot over the counter and into the sink. The bottom of her foot blistered as the cold running water reduced the pain to a mild throb. What was she going to do now? The left side of her head scorched, leaving a noticeable patch of missing hair, and a blister the size of a seedless grape nestled in the middle of her instep. She had to do something. If she didn't work, her rent wasn't paid and she didn't eat.

Inside the tiny bathroom, she reached under the sink and retrieved the scissors. She looked into the mirror and, without a second thought, her wet shoulder-length tresses instantly became a bob. Then she wrapped her hair in a circular motion and sat under the hair dryer for forty-five minutes. Afterward, she wrapped a gauze bandage around her instep, finger combed her new do, and slithered her svelte physique into a black, semi-sheer slip dress once belonging to Camille. This was the only item of Camille's she held onto. Not so much for memory, because she'll never forget Camille, but because it was all Camille owned that held an ounce of class. She felt different tonight. She didn't feel like dressing the role of a low class whore.

# Apple Tree

She took one last glance in the mirror and gave herself final approval. She reached into the hall closet, pulled out her black, full-length Harvé Bernard coat, and wrapped it around her shoulders. She licked her lips, pursed them together and, with a new attitude, she walked out the door and toward her office, the corner of 14th and R Streets.

# Chapter 22

It was unusually mild for a winter night.

Jalisha's dress was black with a low V-shape in the back. The strings in the front of the dress held her breast up toward her chin. Her thick thighs and toned calves peeked through the window-paned fishnet pantyhose. Her ankles wobbled on her black, patent-leather stiletto pumps and her lips were pouting with red lip paint.

She stood on the corner of 14th and R Streets as her thigh protruded from the thigh-high split, her hand propped on her hip. She was a woman on a mission.

The sweet, inviting hum of the cranberry red Mercedes 500 SL convertible, with spinners, pulled curbside. The reflection of the moon bounced off the honey-dipped colored dome, with hazel eyes that pierced through her flesh and caused a wave of heat to rush throughout her. Jalisha glanced over her shoulder. The spinning wheels made her dizzy. She turned on her senses and made sure whoever was in the ride wasn't Metropolitan's finest laying out a trap. She leaned in and took a closer look. The hazel eyes looked familiar.

He leaned over into the passenger seat and let out a long, audible breath. "How much?" His voice was deep and mellow, somewhat soothing.

Jalisha's body stiffened.

"How much?" His voice dropped in volume, but hardened.

She walked slowly toward the Mercedes and slightly bended her knees. She leaned forward, trying to look inside the car. She couldn't believe her eyes. Damn he looks good, she thought to herself.

"Derek, is that you?"

He chuckled. "Are you still charging fifty bucks?"

"Well I'll be damned. What's going on with you?" she asked, taking a step back and admiring the king sitting upon his thrown on wheels. "Looks like you've hit the big time."

"Hey baby girl, long time no see. Naw, I'm working hard, making ends meet, and trying to survive."

He peeped in his rearview mirror. The white cruiser with red, white, and blue markings approached. Derek hopped out of his ride and rushed toward Jalisha.

"Go with the flow," he said, giving her a long warm kiss on the lips.

After breaking their embrace, he reached for the shiny, silver door handle, opened the door, and motioned for her to get in. The cruiser moved right along.

"What was that for?" she asked.

"Didn't want to have to bail you out of jail tonight," he chuckled.

"You wouldn't have to bail me out of jail because I'm not doing anything wrong."

"Oh please, Jalisha. Who do you think you're fooling?"

"What?"

"You honestly want me to believe you're not out here tricking?"

"You can believe what you want."

"That's what I thought," he snickered.

Derek placed the car in drive and pulled away from the curb. The warm night air tousled through Jalisha's new short do.

"Where are we going?" she asked, leaning her head back against the headrest.

Jalisha was really digging the ride and the driver. It had been a minute since she last saw Derek, and he was looking damn good to her too.

"For a ride," he said, glancing toward her. "Are you cold?"

"No, not really."

Derek turned on the heat and then turned up the volume on Jaheim's Put That Woman First.

"So, what's been going on with you, other than the obvious?" he asked in a sarcastic manner.

Jalisha raised her head and looked at him. If looks could kill, his ass would have been running off the road right then. "What the fuck is that suppose to mean? Just because—"

"Calm down, girl. I'm messing with you."

Jalisha cut her eyes at Derek, leaned back against the headrest, and looked up at the stars as the little red jet dashed down 14th Street in the direction of Haines Point.

"So, what's been up?" he asked, attempting to ease a soon-to-be hostile situation.

"Nothing," she responded blankly.

He glanced toward her and rested his hand on her knee. She didn't budge.

"Come on, Lisha. Don't act that way, girl."

"I ain't been up to nothing. doing the same as you, trying to make ends meet and survive. How much you sell to drive this off the lot?"

Derek shook his head in disbelief. "I have a J.O.B., sista."

"What kinda job you have that you could afford this kinda ride?"

"An honest paying job. One you should think about pursuing," he snapped.

Once inside Haines Point, Derek sought out a secluded spot and parked his ride.

"You're still looking good, Lisha," he said. "Let's go for a walk."

"I don't feel like walking."

"Well, I know this isn't 14th Street, but it's a nice night out for walking."

"Now see, fuck you, niggah!"

"I see you haven't changed a bit."

Jalisha sucked her teeth, took a deep sigh, and pulled herself out of the car. She followed Derek to the shoreline and stood beside him, her finger slightly touching his.

"Why are you still doing this, Lisha?"

"What else am I going to do?"

"You could get a decent, legal job."

"There ain't a decent, legal job that's gonna pay me what I make in one night."

"What you're doing isn't safe..."

"I know you aren't talking about being safe, driving around in an expensive ass car..."

"I have a job, sista. I went back to school, got my degree, and I don't have to sell my ass to make ends meet," he snapped. Then he straightened his shoulders and leaned back. "Listen, I didn't bring you out here to argue."

"Why did you bring me out here?"

"To try and put you on the right track."

"I don't understand," she said, whisking the hair from her brow.

"I saw you a few weeks ago, turning your tricks. You are too good for that, Lisha. I have always been fond of you and, while I am no knight in shining armor, I do want to help you get out of the game. That is, if you want to."

Jalisha faced Derek and smiled as a tear slowly fell down her cheek.

"I don't know anything else," she cried. "Do you know about Corine?"

"I heard about what happened and I'm so sorry. I know how close you two were."

Derek moved in closer and took Jalisha by the hand. He entwined his fingers with hers as the heat from their longing warmed them.

"Jalisha, I've missed you. I have been trying to find you ever since you left Lincoln Heights. No one knew where you were or how to find you."

"After Corine's death, I decided there was no reason for me to be there. Besides, I was tired of living in the projects. I wanted something different out of life. I wanted a change."

"What you're doing...this is different."

"In a way, yes. I live in a different neighborhood..."

"That's not what I meant. You said you wanted something different out of life. There's nothing different you're doing, only in a different location."

"It pays my bills," she said as they gazed into each other's eyes. Not even Bon Jovi could break the thick silence between them.

# *Chapter* 23

Jalisha rose out of bed feeling refreshed. For the first time in years, she had not spent the night on her knees, her back, or in a stranger's car. She felt different and seeing Derek excited her. She enjoyed being in his presence the night before. She could not recall the last time she had a conversation with anyone except for herself. After Corine's death, she became a loner. She had no friends and she trusted no one. That was the way she wanted it. That was the way she liked it. But last night, she felt like she was on a real date.

After Haines Point, they drove to Georgetown to Manhattan Seafood Bar & Grill where Derek introduced her to grilled salmon, clams casino, white wine and a jazz quartet. She loved every minute of it. To her, this was the good life. They talked about everything under the sun, including his job as a Paralegal for a prestigious law firm in downtown Washington, DC. He told her of his dreams of going back to school for his law degree and one day becoming a successful attorney, like the great Johnny Cochran. "That brother is admired by all," he had said. "While everybody else wants to be like Mike, I wanna be like Johnny."

Jalisha's feet pressed against the cold linoleum kitchen floor as she reached into the refrigerator for the carton of Florida orange juice and a pint of cottage cheese. After placing the items on the countertop, she opened the cupboard and pulled out a can of Delmonte's fruit cocktail. Cottage cheese with fruit cocktail was her favorite breakfast. She pulled a clean bowl from the dishwasher and a spoon from the drawer. As she spooned the cottage cheese into the bowl, the phone rang. She reached for the phone and nestled it in her neck, between her chin and shoulder.

"Hello."

"This is Derek."

Her voice softened. "Hi there."

"Are you busy?"

"No, having breakfast."

"Oh, I guess I'm too late. I was calling to ask you out to breakfast..."

She cut him off quick, fast, and in a hurry. "I can still go!" She sounded desperate and she did not give a rat's ass.

"All right then," he chuckled. "I can pick you up in an hour."

"I'll meet you downstairs," she sighed. "My place is a mess," she added bashfully.

"See you in an hour."

Jalisha was so excited, she forgot to say bye and hung up in Derek's face. She tossed everything into the refrigerator, even the unopened can of fruit cocktail and dashed for the bathroom, where she drew herself a warm bath. as she was about to drop her robe to the floor, a knock sounded at the door. She quizzically looked over her shoulder and slowly walked to the door. Her head tilted with question marks all over her face. Who could this be, she wondered. She looked through the peephole, but could not make out the blurry image.

"May I help you," she asked through the door.

"Yes, Ma'am, I have a delivery for Jalisha Thomas."

Hesitant to open the door, she asked, "What kind of delivery?"

Jalisha was an avid news watcher. She knew about people knocking on doors, disguising themselves as a repairman, or the like, to get into the house and do God only knows what to you. She remembered reading about the man who disguised himself as a PEPCO representative. as the woman was opening her door, the man stormed inside her home and raped her repeatedly. Physically, the woman survived, but mentally she will never be the same. What frightened Jalisha was the fact this all took place three blocks from her apartment building. That was enough for her, which was why she kept a loaded .22 caliber at the top of the hall closet beside the front door. She was prepared for whatever came her way, especially considering her profession.

"Delivery from Lexington Florists, Ma'am."

She slowly opened the door. The sweet aroma of roses smacked her in the face.

"Oh my God!" she exclaimed. "Who are they from?"

"Don't know, Ma'am. Could you please sign here?"

Jalisha signed on the dotted line and slammed the door without giving the delivery person a tip. She did not know any better. Etiquette and class, respectively, was not her forte.

She carefully sat the vase-filled bouquet of a dozen red roses, with fern and baby's breath, on the coffee table and snatched the card from the bouquet.

# Apple Tree

*Thank you for a lovely evening.*
*I hope to share many more with you.*
*Always, Derek*

Jalisha could not believe her eyes. She had never received flowers before. *I'll take them to Corey tomorrow,* she thought. *She will absolutely love them!* She giggled, danced, and jumped around. Derek had made her day.

## *Chapter 24*

As promised, Jalisha sat Indian-style at Corine's gravesite.

"Corey, do you like them?" she asked, arranging the roses. "You won't believe who gave them to me. Yeah, Derek! Can you believe that?"

She took a deep sigh, stretched her arms before her, and clasped her hands together. She cracked her knuckles and rested her chin on her hands.

"I know it's been a while since I was last here. You know how things are. It is not that I do not want to come and see you, but it is hard for me, Corey, to see you here and not with me, where we can talk and laugh as we used to do. It is because of me you are here dead. Actually, it is because of Camille. I'll never forgive…well, that's all water under the bridge now."

The cold and dampness from the ground was beginning to seep through her denim pants. She pulled herself upright and hunched her shoulders.

"I miss you something awful, Corey." She looked around at the other gravesites and said, "You have the prettiest flowers out here, Corey." She smiled, shoving her hands in her pockets. "Well, I have to go now, little sister. I'll come back to visit you again."

Jalisha leaned over and pressed her hand against

the headstone. She closed her eyes and wept briefly before she said, "I love you, Corey."

As Jalisha walked away, an eerie feeling overcame her. She looked over her shoulder toward the gravesite and said, "I'm going to get out of the business."

# *Chapter 25*

As Jalisha walked down the muddy hill of the cemetery, she came to an abrupt halt. The chilly wind blew through her, causing her to shiver. However, the sight of Derek warmed her heart.

"Hey you," she smiled, walking toward him. "What are you doing here?"

"Hey back at ya'." He winked and took her into an embrace.

"What are you doing here?" she asked once again.

"I don't know. I was driving and something drew me here."

"Must've been me," she flirted.

"Must have been." His thoughts wandered up the hill. "Corine?" he asked.

Jalisha solemnly responded, "Yes."

"Do you come here often?"

"No. It's been a minute."

"Do you mind?" he asked, looking up the hill.

"No. I am sure she would like it. You know, she liked you."

Derek chuckled, clasped his hand with hers, and led her up the hill.

Jalisha became hesitant when she realized the roses Derek sent her were scattered all over Corine's gravesite. She gently pulled back.

"What's wrong?"

"Well, I…I'm sorry, Derek."

"Huh?"

"The roses you sent me…I put them on Corey's grave."

Derek's smile warmed her heart. He pulled her into him and kissed her on the neck.

"Lady, you are wonderful. What a wonderful gesture."

"You mean you don't mind?"

"Why should I mind?"

Jalisha shrugged her shoulders and stared at Corine's headstone.

"Are you okay?" Derek asked, pressing his hand against her lower back. Jalisha shuddered. "Baby…"

"Yes," she said, struggling to regain composure, "I'm fine. I …," she stuttered, the feeling of guilt swept through her. "It should've been me instead," she cried. "How could someone be so cruel?"

Derek pulled her into him. She nestled her face into his neck and exhaled a deep moan. Her throat was dry. Her heart ached profusely. Her sense of loss was beyond tears.

The morning she found Corine sprawled out and lifeless still haunted her. She cried for help, but her cries went unheard. Even amongst the group of people who stood around and made nasty, snide comments: "serves the tramp right" and "no different than that nasty ass mama" or "that's a damn shame." When the paramedics arrived, it was too late. The coroner concluded Corine had bled to death due to a severed clitoris.

"This is why I haven't been to visit Corey in such a

long time. I cannot handle it. It's been seven years since her death and…"

Derek silenced her with his index finger pressed against her lips.

"But…"

Derek briskly shook his head. "No, Lisha. You can't keep blaming yourself."

"But, if I…"

"No buts, darling. Listen, you have to take stock in yourself. It is time for you to change your life, Lisha. What happened to Corey could happen to you."

"But she was a child. Who would do that to a child?"

"A sick motherfucker, that's who," Derek snapped becoming irritated with the conversation. "Hey, I've got an idea. Let's grab some dinner."

"I can't. I have to work tonight."

Sudden anger lit his eyes. "Damnit, Lisha!"

Jalisha jumped a mile from the ground and stumbled backward.

"Do you have a death wish?"

"No, I don't!" she yelled back at him.

"Do you like opening your legs and swallowing shit from niggahs you don't know shit about?"

"Derek, you know I don't. Nevertheless, I have to make a living. I don't…"

"Cut the bullshit, Lisha," he growled. He walked closer to her and leaned in. She could smell the Doublemint gum that swished around in his mouth. "I care about you. I care what happens to you. I don't want you doing this anymore," he pleaded.

"I have no choice," she whined.

"Nonsense! We all have choices. You tricking on the corner at night is your choice."

"I can't do anything else! Leave me the fuck alone!"

Jalisha stormed off down the hill. Derek called out to her several times until she was out of sight.

# Chapter 26

Jalisha sat on the countertop in the kitchen, sipping on a diet Pepsi. The events of the day played over in her mind, especially what went down with Derek. She did not like him telling her what she should and should not do. However, she hoped she did not chase him away. She had never had anyone to care for her or about what she did. Not even Camille showed an ounce of concern.

Camille did not care about her damn self. Not even enough to keep up with her hygiene. After her death, rumor had it several men she had met had all contracted HIV and she was the carrier and did not even know it.

"Oh well," she sighed, then gave a resigned shrug.

Jalisha hopped off the counter and rummaged through the freezer. She hardly cooked, so everything in the freezer was…God only knows how old.

Her mind constantly reminisced about the other night she was with Derek at Haines Point. The anticipation of seeing him again gnawed at her and was almost unbearable. Did she mess up today with Derek? She was quite nasty to him, but he was not Mr. Nice Guy either. What he said was true and she knew it. She needed to get out of the game, but she was in too deep. She possessed no other skills. After Camille died, she and Corey stopped going to school. The public school system was so overcrowded, the girls fell through the cracks, and no one missed them.

Although seeing him aroused old fears and uncertainty from Lincoln Heights, she had a much stronger guard up now and decided to search for the crumpled up piece of paper he gave her the other night with his phone numbers. She dialed his cell number and patiently waited through four loud rings.

"Speak ya peace," he answered, the radio blaring around him.

"Derek?"

"Yeah. Who's this?"

"This is Lisha."

"Oh hey…sup?" Disappointment settled in his voice.

When she tried to speak, her voice wavered. "Derek, I owe you an apology from earlier today."

"Don't worry about it," he said, his voice softening.

"I hate the way I felt afterward and I don't want to run you off…"

"I'm not going anywhere, Lisha. Know that."

Her shoulders relaxed. "I'm glad. What are you doing?"

"Nothing, riding around."

"Would you like to come over?"

"I thought you had to work tonight."

"I'm calling in sick," she chuckled. "How about eight o'clock? I'll fix some dinner."

"I'll bring the wine."

"I prefer Crown Royal," she said bashfully.

He gave a short chuckle and released the call.

# Chapter 27

In all her years, she did not know the first thing about dating, let alone romance. She frantically flipped through Essence and Ebony magazines and, of course, they were no help. She turned on the television in hopes of finding something that would give her a hint. Nothing. Finally, she gave up and plopped down on her sofa.

What am I doing? she thought. I can't woo this damn man.

She could feel disappointment creeping up on her, but she decided she wasn't going to go there. She was determined to do something right for a change.

She grabbed the pad and pen from the sofa table and began to jot down thoughts of how she would like to be treated. She remembered the scene from Two Can Play That Game when Vivica A. Fox immersed herself in a warm, inviting bubble bath. She jotted down:

1. Bubble bath with a glass of wine.

One of the things she's always wanted to do was to have a massage. One of her regulars was nice enough to give her body and massage oils from Bath and Body Works for Christmas. However, she never once used them.

2. Body massage.

What about dinner? She didn't have a clue as to

what she was going to prepare, so she flipped through
the Betty Crocker cookbook she picked up at the thrift
shop, with hopes of one day preparing a gourmet meal.
Jalisha couldn't cook worth a hot damn. Perusing the
pages, she stumbled across a menu that appeared
romantic.

3. Crab Imperial and a garden salad.

While this menu was not as romantic as she'd like it
to be, it's all she can afford to muster up at this time.
Besides, the recipe was easy.

The last thing she needed was candles. She would
pick those up from Dollar General.

Jalisha completed her grocery list, grabbed her purse,
and stormed out the door, rushing to the Safeway. She
had four hours to make everything perfect. She didn't
know how, but she was going to make this a night
neither she nor Derek would forget.

With an hour left, she mixed the ingredients for the
Crab Imperial into a ceramic casserole bowl she picked
up from the Dollar General and turned the oven to
350° F.

She glanced at her watch. "Damn," she mumbled
and wondered what else there was to do. With so little
time left, she still needed to get herself together.

She darted toward the bathroom and turned on the
shower. She kicked off her slippers and slipped out of
her red velour sweats, allowing them to fall around her
ankles. She pulled off the matching hooded top and
dropped it to the floor. She stepped into the shower
and immersed herself under the stream. She grabbed
for the Dove body wash and began lathering herself.
She was enjoying the warmth of the water mixed with

her touch, when she realized, through all of the excitement, she had forgotten to remove her lace panty and bra ensemble.

She stepped out of the shower and wrapped herself in a white, extra thick terrycloth robe. She wrapped her hair in a towel and proceeded to brush her teeth. With a mouth full of Crest toothpaste, a knock at the door startled her. She quickly rinsed her mouth and used the back of her hand to wipe away the leftover toothpaste from the corners of her mouth.

Standing on the tips of her toes, she peeped through the peephole and took a step backward.

"Oh shit!" she quietly exclaimed. "He's early."

She looked at the clock. He wasn't early. She took the longest shower known to man.

"Uh, just a minute," she yelled through the door.

She quickly opened the door and sprinted toward her bedroom. "I'll be with you in a minute," she yelled at him.

Derek slowly walked through the door and looked around Jalisha's apartment. He didn't expect her place to be so neat. Actually, he didn't know what to expect. Maybe he was expecting a replica of Camille. Maybe he was expecting it to look like The Best Little Whorehouse in DC. However, what he didn't expect was to turn around and find Jalisha standing before him in a classy, full-length eggplant satin, strapless gown. Physically, Jalisha hadn't lost her figure. She still had the body of a sixteen-year-old. Her new haircut made her look mature, classy, and desirable.

"Wow!" was all Derek could muster.

Jalisha smiled and lowered her head.

"Baby, don't do that," he said, raising her chin with his index finger. "You look radiant."

"Thank you," she whispered.

"Thank you," he said, bringing her face to his, "for being back in my life."

Their lips met. With one hand, he caressed her face, while the other roamed her backside.

Jalisha began to feel funny. It was a feeling she'd never felt before. It was warm, tingly, and satisfying. She felt dampness between her thighs.

She pulled herself into him, caressing her abdomen with his pelvis. His love grew as she stroked the back of his head.

Derek leaned back against the wall. His pants were heavy from his arousal.

"Girl, what are you doing to me?"

Jalisha took her tongue and swirled in a circular motion behind his earlobe.

"Damn, baby," he panted. Her left cheek filled the palm of his hand.

Jalisha grabbed hold of his earlobe and gently nibbled while her hand wandered to his midsection. She stroked his stomach and made her way to his belt. After she unbuckled his belt, she unzipped his pants and felt around his abdomen and inside his boxers.

Derek let out a slight bitch moan.

Jalisha smiled to herself, wrapped her petite fingers around his love, and caressed his softness, feeling it grow rapidly.

"Damn, girl," Derek moaned, massaging the back of her neck.

Jalisha released his earlobe and bowed down before

him. She looked up at him and smiled because she knew she had him. The trick pulled the oldest trick in the book. She allowed his swollen member to rest in the warmth and moisture of her mouth.

Derek inhaled deeply and palmed the back of her head, pulling her closer into him.

Jalisha was careful not to blow Derek the way she blew her clients; fast, rough and quick. No, with Derek, she gave him oral pleasure he'd never quite experienced.

Inside a pair of Timberlands, Derek's toes started to curl.

Jalisha could feel his body intensify as his dick stroked the back of her throat.

"Aww shit, baby! Damn!"

Without warning, Derek filled her throat with a mound of seeds.

Jalisha felt herself creaming. She took him by the hand and led him to her bedroom.

At the doorway, Derek stopped, turned Jalisha toward him, grabbed her face, and brought her mouth to his.

Jalisha felt weak.

Derek's hands left her face and wandered down to her lean shoulders, massaging them. He felt along her waist, stopping at her zipper. Her dress fell around her freshly painted red toes. He took her in his arms, gently laid her on the bed, and took a step backward.

Jalisha reached out for him.

He smiled and began to unbutton his shirt, giving her a private show. He still looked the way she remembered. Memories of their first sexual encounter frolicked through her mind. She closed her eyes and reached for his love.

"This is your night," he whispered, gently brushing her hand away.

Derek knelt down beside the bed and took inventory.

Like an automatic door, Jalisha's legs slowly opened.

"Spread your pussy for me," he said.

She exposed the swelling between her legs.

Derek leaned in, licked his lips, and feathered his tongue across her swollen knot.

She flinched and gasped deeply.

He pressed the palms of his hands under her thighs and pushed her legs to her chest, slightly raising her hips. His tongue explored her southern exposure, absorbing the tiny stream of cream.

Jalisha felt herself tremble as he nursed her swollen clitoris.

"Ahh, don't stop!" she panted. "Don't you dare stop!"

She was feeling pleasure she never felt before. After all, performing oral sex was always her job. Not once had one of her tricks offered to please her.

"Mmm, girl, you are like a faucet," Derek teased.

Jalisha couldn't respond. He was sucking the breath out of her.

"Don't hold back, Mama."

Jalisha briskly shook her head from side to side. Her hand patted the bed; she couldn't breathe.

"Let it go, Lish."

"I feel…," she stuttered, "like I have to pee."

"I know, baby. Let it go."

She relaxed her muscles, releasing a powerful flow of cream. She inhaled deeply and exhaled briskly.

"That was good, baby," he said, patting her on the hips.

# *Chapter 28*

Jalisha laid sprawled across the bed in a deep sleep. Unknowingly, she smiled at the thought of the events that had taken place the night before. She placed her hands between her warm thighs and deeply sighed. She stretched out her foot and kicked a lump in the bed beside her.

What the hell? she thought.

She looked down and saw Derek lying across the foot of the bed, naked as a jaybird. She lifted her head, looked around the room, and then down at herself. She was naked too. She plopped her head down and tried to figure out why she was missing her clothes and why in the hell was Derek naked and ass up at the foot of her bed?

The Hypnotic mixed with Hennessy to form a green concoction called The Incredible Hulk must have knocked her out cold. She remembered the wonderful dinner she prepared that Derek inhaled. She remembered how she worked him, causing his toes to curl. She remembered experiencing her first orgasm that still had her feeling sensations throughout – not to mention the throbbing between her legs had been going on for the last six hours or so. Nevertheless, for the life of her, she couldn't remember actually having intercourse with Derek.

She pulled back the leopard-print comforter and whispered, "Derek, get under the covers."

Derek raised his head and gazed at her, trying to focus.

"Come on. Get under the covers before you catch cold."

Derek looked around and then at himself. He had a look of bewilderment on his face and crawled beneath the covers where he nestled beside Jalisha. He grabbed her around her waist.

"What happened to our clothes?" he chuckled.

"I've been trying to figure that one out myself."

"Damn, I don't remember…did we have…did we make…," he trailed off, not wanting to say the S word.

"I don't know what we did."

They both laughed.

"Damn, I guess our drinks were too strong, huh?" he said, pulling her close into him.

"Yeah, I guess so."

He nestled his lips in her neck and gently kissed her, causing the hair on her neck to stand. She purred from the stroke of his tongue. She tilted her head into him.

"You like that?" he asked in a soft whisper, sending a sensual shock between her legs.

Derek slid his hand between her thighs. She gripped his hand tightly.

"Hey, why so tight?" he asked, puzzled.

"I think I have to pee."

Derek removed his hand, pulled back the covers, and motioned for her to get out of bed.

Her firm body jetted to the bathroom and closed the door.

"I want to come in," Derek said, standing at the door with the comforter wrapped around him like a towel.

"Why?" she asked, irritated because the impending stream came to an abrupt halt.

"Why not?"

"This is private time. Thank you very much!"

"I want to share everything with you, Lisha," he whined. "Come on, let me in!"

"Oh all right, damn."

She leaned forward and opened the door.

"You look sexy sitting on the toilet with your legs open like that."

"Nasty ass," she chuckled.

"I thought you had to pee."

"I do, but I can't pee while you're standing there."

"Why not?"

"Derek, will you please get real?" she smirked.

"I am real," he said, walking up on her.

"What are you doing?"

Derek leaned in and placed his hand between her legs.

"Derek?"

"I'm going to help you…"

"You're going to get the fuck out of here!"

She grabbed his hand and forcefully shoved him toward the door, which turned him on more. He moved in closer and forced his hand between her closed legs, prying them open.

"Derek!" she said playfully. "Stop it!"

The flickering of his finger to her clit made her suppress the urge to urinate.

"Give it to me, baby," he whispered. His minty breath from the gum he held in his mouth all night warmed her face.

He forced the urge out of her. She rained all over his finger.

"Eww, now go wash your hands!"

He looked down at her and smiled. "You liked that, didn't you?"

She smiled. She wanted him to leave so she could at least wipe her ass in private.

Derek reached for the toilet paper.

"Umm, what are you doing, Derek?"

"Umm, I think I am going to wipe you."

"Umm, I think not!" she snapped. "You done lost your mind for sure."

"Now, I didn't think you were inhibited, Lisha."

"What the fuck is that suppose to mean?" she barked.

"Nothing…"

"Oh, it means something!" Without wiping, she rose up and pulled her underwear around her waist.

"Look, don't…"

"Oh no, motherfucker, don't you look me!"

"Hold up now, Lisha. You're getting carried away and I don't like your tone."

"Do you think I give a fuck what you don't like? This is my motherfuckin' house. You don't like it. Get the fuck out!"

Derek squared his shoulders, took a deep sigh, and left the bathroom with Jalisha on his heels.

"I want to know what you meant by that comment of yours."

"It was nothing."

"Oh, it was something. Tell me what the fuck you meant!"

"Jalisha, you really need to stop cussing. You sound more and more like your mother."

Jalisha took a deep inhale.

"Well, the apple doesn't fall far from the tree, motherfucker!"

"Fine!" he yelled in his deep baritone voice. "You want to know what I meant?"

Jalisha placed her hand on her hip and briskly nodded her head.

"I figured since you were out here selling your ass for cash, you would go to any lengths! Hell, if you sucking on a stranger's dick, then my finger swirling in your piss should be a piece of cake!"

Without warning, Jalisha's hand came across Derek's face in a fit of rage.

Derek stood his ground. He didn't budge, although he felt like knocking her into next week. However, he didn't believe in putting his hands on women.

"How dare you talk to me like…"

"Like what? Like the whore you are?" he snarled. "I thought I could change you. I was wrong."

"Yes, you were! Accept me for me or leave me the fuck alone."

"I can't accept my woman being a whore."

"When did we decide I was your woman?"

Derek shook his head and slipped on his pants.

"I am my own woman, Derek. You can't change me. I am what I am."

He gazed at her in defeat.

"Yes, I guess you are. Take care, Lisha."

Jalisha watched as Derek walked out of her life.

# *Chapter 29*

Jalisha cried as she thought about the mean things she spewed at Derek. Over the years, so much hatred had grown within her. With every passing day, she mirrored Camille.

Jalisha took a deep sigh of defeat, hugged her pillow beneath her, and closed her eyes. Mentally, she was tired and needed to rest. Which would explain why she quickly drifted off to sleep, and into another space and time.

"Girl, what is wrong with you?" Corine asked, bouncing up and down on Jalisha's bed.

"Corey?" Jalisha shot up in the bed.

"I've missed you so much, Lisha," Corine said, crossing her legs Indian style.

"You look good, Corey. I can't believe it's you."

"Yes, it's me."

"Oh my God...am I?"

"No, you're not dead, just me," Corine giggled.

Jalisha reached out her hand toward Corine.

"You haven't changed a bit, Corey, you still look fourteen."

"Yes, well, that's one good thing about being dead...you don't age," she laughed.

Corine looked around the bedroom.

"Still at it, huh, Lish?" She took a deep sigh. "Please

don't end up used up and no good to anyone like Camille. By the way, I've yet to run into our mother. I guess she was detoured to the basement."

"To the base…" Jalisha caught herself. It dawned on her what Corey meant. "Heaven is a big place. I'm sure you'll run into her."

"No. I doubt it. Besides, I don't want to run into her. Look at how we turned out, Lish. Nevertheless, we have to forgive. I've forgiven her, but I'll never forget."

Jalisha lowered her head.

"I'm so lonely, Corey. I have no friends, no family…"

"What about Derek?"

"What about him, and how do you know about him anyway?"

Corine chuckled. "Another perk about being," she pointed upward, "up there is being able to keep your eye on the ones you love."

"I always knew you were my angel." Jalisha smiled.

"I'm always with you, Lisha. Know that." Corine sighed. "Well, I don't have much time, so let me get to why I'm here."

Jalisha straightened her shoulders and began to listen intently.

"Jalisha, that man cares for you, and always has ever since back in the day."

"I really care for him, too."

"Well, act like it and stop acting like a brat. Trust me, Lisha, Derek is going to be good for you. Go to him."

Jalisha lowered her head and allowed the tear to fall, staining the sheet.

"Well, big sis. I have to run. I love you, Lisha, and I'm keeping my eye on you."

"I love you too, Corey," Jalisha cried.

Corey stood to her feet. "Oh, and Lisha?"

"Yes?"

"Always follow your heart. You don't want to do this anymore. Take Derek by the hand and allow him to lead you out of destruction."

"How did you get so wise?" Jalisha asked, smiling up at Corine.

Corine rolled her eyes upward. "I have a wonderful teacher."

"But I don't know what to do," Jalisha blurted out.

"Yeah right. Work what Camille gave you, but be classy about it." She smiled a warm smile. "I've got to go now, Lisha. I love you...and love the hair!"

Jalisha woke in a cold sweat. She slowly looked around the room. She could feel Corine's presence. She could even smell her. She stretched her arms above her head and smiled.

"This is going to be a good day," she sighed.

# Chapter 30

The next day, Jalisha took matters into her own hands. It was time for her to do something she'd never done before: Apologize.

Knock. Knock. Knock.

Jalisha stood in the chilly November air hoping Derek was home. She didn't see his car parked in front of his house.

Knock. Knock. Knock.

Jalisha tightened the belt around her beige, full-length trench coat.

Knock. Knock. Knock.

No answer.

Jalisha turned to walk away when she heard the turning of the lock.

"What brings you here?" Derek asked, holding open the storm door and motioning for her to come in.

Jalisha stepped into the foyer. "I wanted to apologize for yesterday."

"It's all right, Lisha. You coming here is apologizing enough."

Derek reached for her coat.

Jalisha untied the belt around her waist and allowed her trench coat to fall open.

Derek gasped.

Jalisha slipped out of her trench and revealed a red chiffon, trimmed in lace, two-piece negligee. Her lean legs were shimmering from baby oil. Her red painted toes enhanced the three-inch heels with a thin strap around the ankle.

Derek was breathless.

Jalisha stood before Derek with confidence. She was a woman on a mission. She was going to get her man back.

"You are so beautiful…like a ray of sunshine," Derek whispered.

"Well, don't let all of this beauty go to waste," Jalisha said, smiling.

Derek took her by the hand and led her up the stairs to his bedroom.

The tall, four-poster bed draped in a teal green duvet was inviting.

Without a word, Derek led her to the bed, palmed her face, and tasted her lips. He dropped his hands to her breast and began tweaking her nipples, feeling them swell from her excitement. Her fragrance, Alfred Sung's Pure, aroused him more.

Derek took a step backward and gazed at her beauty. He slid the straps of her negligee off her shoulders, allowing it to fall down around her ankles and drape on her red toes. He dropped to his knees and pulled her toward him. He stroked his tongue around her belly button and down toward her sex as he palmed her perky breast.

Jalisha threw her head back. Aroused now, she drew him closer to her. Her moans were deep and sensual.

Derek kissed around her sex and inserted his tongue between her lips, where her swollen bud throbbed.

"Derek," she moaned, deep and intensified.

Jalisha fell back onto the bed and spread her legs, raising them above his head.

"Oooh, yes!" she exclaimed with short, dry pants.

Derek sucked, licked, and gnawed until Jalisha's body stiffened and convulsed. She expelled a sharp shriek of pleasure.

Derek stood to his feet and Jalisha watched as he slowly removed his clothes. He positioned himself on top of her and inserted himself between her legs.

Her body heaved into his as she grabbed him around his waist.

"Ummm," he moaned with pleasure. "Damn, girl, you've got some good pussy."

Jalisha slowly moved her hips into Derek's abdomen, slightly tilting upward. Her muscles contracted, gripping his manhood. Derek lost control. It was flesh against flesh, man against woman. It was on. Who was going to fuck whom the best?

"You trying to hook a brotha," Derek said between pants. "Umm, hum," he grunted.

"Whose dick is it?" Jalisha asked, smiling up at him, all the while tightening her muscles and leaving her invisible imprint. The next time he sexed anyone else, it wouldn't be the same.

Derek couldn't speak, only mustering a slight moan.

Together, they found the tempo that bound their bodies together. The pleasure was explosive, but she needed more intensity.

"Give it to me," she demanded, palming his ass and pushing him deeper into her. "Yeah, that's it. That's it, baby."

Derek buried his head in her neck.

She grabbed hold of his ear and began sucking his earlobe.

His strokes became fierce, yet gentle.

"That's it, Derek. Don't stop, baby. Don't you stop fucking me!"

She felt him throb within her.

"Oh, shit," he expelled from deep within. "Shit!"

Derek's face distorted. His defenses weakened.

Jalisha wrapped her legs around his waist and felt his love flow through her like warm honey.

Contentment and peace flowed through them as they cuddled and drifted off to sleep.

# *Chapter 31*

Jalisha tiptoed to the bathroom, careful not to wake Derek. After all, he was exhausted and she was damn proud of herself. She worked his ass and worked it good!

She lowered the toilet seat and straddled it. She looked around the bathroom and noticed how clean it was. No soap scum. No pubic hair on the floor. No cluttered sink. She peeked in the medicine cabinet. Every bottle was in alphabetical order and lined up perfectly.

"What a neat freak," she mumbled to herself.

She flushed the toilet and turned on the shower. She pulled a towel from the shelf above the toilet and wrapped it around her hair. Once the water temperature was to her liking, she climbed into the shower, immersed herself under the downpour, and took a sigh of satisfaction. For the first time, she felt complete.

# *Chapter* 32

She heard something. It sounded like voices, but Jalisha wasn't quite sure. She turned off the shower and quietly pulled back the blue and gray striped shower curtain. Her wet toes meshed with the navy blue shag carpet that was part of the bathroom ensemble. She pulled the towel off her head and wrapped it around her torso, toga style. She crept to the door and slowly rested her hand on the knob. Gently turning the knob, she cracked the door enough to hear what was going on.

"Your cell has been turned off all night, Derek!" The woman's voice carried from the foyer to the upstairs bathroom where Jalisha was hiding out.

"My phone was not off," Derek responded in a calm manner. "You need to lower your voice."

"Yes, it was! Do you think I'm an idiot? Every single time I dialed your number, your phone did not ring. Instead, it went directly into voicemail. That means it was turned off!" she yelled louder.

"I don't work for Sprint, so I can't begin to tell you what the fuck was going on with the phone, Rita!"

"And why are you standing here with no fucking clothes on?" Rita took a step back and glared at Derek.

"What?" he asked.

She squared her shoulders and stepped closer, smelling his breath.

SMACK!

"Motherfucker! That ain't my goddamn pussy on your breath!" Rita looked up the staircase. She inched past Derek.

Derek grabbed her by the wrist. "Where are you going, Rita?"

Rita faced Derek and looked down at his hand wrapped around her wrist. "Upstairs," she replied through clinched teeth. "Let go of me, Derek."

"You don't need to go upstairs. You need to leave."

"You putting me out, Derek?"

Derek's voice was silent, but his eyes spoke volumes.

"Why can't I go upstairs, Derek?"

"I want you to leave, Rita. I'm asking you nicely."

Rita jerked her wrist away from his grasp. "Fine! You want me to leave, fine. But let me tell you this, Derek. If I leave this house, I'm never coming back." She adjusted her weight. "Now, you're going to lose me for a one night stand?"

"Baby, you do what you have to do," he responded nonchalantly.

Rita lowered her head and appeared to have given in to defeat.

Derek leaned over and opened the door. "Bye, Rita. Look, I'll call you later. Okay?"

Rita raised her head and stared at him. "I'm not giving you up that easy," she said and sprinted up the stairs like Marion Jones. Rita hit the top landing in lightning speed.

Derek sprinted behind her, but he wasn't fast enough.

Rita barged into Derek's bedroom and came to an

abrupt halt at Jalisha's negligee sprawled across the floor. Jalisha's scent filled the air.

"Where is she? I can smell the whore! Bring your ass out here, bitch. I know you're in here!"

Jalisha took a deep breath, slowly closed the bathroom door, and locked it.

Rita was jolted by the sound of the bathroom door locking. She made a beeline for the bathroom and came face to face with Derek. She reached over his shoulder and banged on the door. "Get your ass out here! You big enough to fuck my man, be big enough to face his woman!"

"Rita, I want you to leave. NOW!"

The harshness of Derek's voice caused her to jump. Tears welled in her eyes. "How could you do this to me. . .to us?"

"There is no us, and you did it to yourself, remember?"

"But baby. . ."

"Rita, my patience is running thin. If you don't leave, I will call the cops."

"Derek, I love you."

"Damn, you desperate bitch, he said leave!" Jalisha yelled from inside the bathroom.

"Lisha, chill with that!" Derek shot back.

"Watch your back, bitch."

"You better watch yours!" Jalisha giggled at the Rita making a damn fool out of herself at the expense of some niggah.

"Fuck you, bitch!" Rita yelled at Jalisha. "And fuck you too, Derek! I don't need this shit. I don't need you! Humph, you think you're the only one who has been all up in this pussy, niggah. Hell no! I gotta man who treats me right. Fuck you!"

WHAM!

Derek's balled up fist landed Rita to the floor. "Get the fuck out of my house and don't you ever bring your tired ass back here. You understand me?" His poisonous venom weakened her.

Rita pulled herself up onto her hands and knees and crawled toward the steps. She used the handrail to bring herself upright. She took one last look at Derek and descended to the foyer. "Your loss, motherfucker!" she yelled as the door slammed behind her.

"Good ridden," he mumbled.

# Chapter 33

"I'm sorry you had to witness that."

Jalisha stood numb as she listened to Derek apologize for knocking the shit out of Rita.

"Lisha, you hear me?"

Jalisha looked at Derek and for a minute, was not sure if she recognized him anymore.

"What's wrong, baby?" he asked, grasping her shoulders and bringing her into him.

Jalisha looked down at this grasp and took a quick step backward. "Do you always do that?" she asked in a low whisper.

"Do what?"

"Hit on women."

Derek took a deep sigh and propped his hand on his hip. "No, baby, I don't. Rita pushed my hand. . ."

"You didn't have to hit her."

"Things were getting out of hand, Jalisha. I won't let her come up in my house and regulate. Besides, she was coming after you."

"I can handle myself."

Derek pulled Jalisha into him and kissed her on the cheek. "I'm sorry. . ."

"Why didn't you tell me you had a girlfriend?"

"She's not my girl."

"Then who is she?"

"A crazy bitch, that's who," he chuckled.

Jalisha wasn't amused.

"Aww come on, baby."

Jalisha turned away from him.

"Hey, Rita is a broad I would fuck from time to time. That's it, Lisha. She don't mean shit to me."

"Well, it's evident she doesn't see it that way, Derek," she snapped. "Look, I'm down with whatever with you, but I don't want any drama, especially drama from a bitch."

"I hear you," he nodded.

"Uh huh, so if I am going to be in your life, I will be the only one or I won't be at all."

Derek rested his hands on his hips and zoned out, deep in thought.

"Derek? Do you hear me talking to you?"

Derek tilted his head to the side, a questionable look flashed across his face.

"Well?" she demanded.

"All right, Lisha, I hear you loud and clear. If that's what you want, I don't have a problem with that. However, since we are placing ultimatums here, I have one for you."

Jalisha folded her arms cross her chest and exhaled. Tit for tat shit, she thought to herself.

"Now, let me make sure I have this right. You are asking me to be exclusive with you, right?"

Jalisha shifted her weight irritably. "Uh huh."

"Well, then if that is what you want, then you are going to stop tricking, right?"

"Derek, you are asking me to give up my livelihood."

"No, I'm not. If we are going to be exclusive, then you shouldn't be seeing anyone else."

"I won't be seeing anyone else. It's my job. If I don't work, I don't live."

"Then get another job," he demanded.

"Derek, this is plain crazy. How am I going to get another job? Doing what?"

"Anything…"

"I have no other skills!" she yelled out of frustration.

"Jalisha, you can answer a phone, can't you?"

"Well, yes, of course I can."

"Fine, then get a job as a receptionist."

"A receptionist?"

"Yep," he nodded. "As a matter of fact, I believe we will have an opening at my job soon. I can put in a good word for you."

Jalisha pressed her fingers against her throbbing temples. She couldn't believe what he was asking her to do, but she could understand though. After all, she surely wouldn't want her man seeing other women. Moreover, it looked as though Derek would now officially be her man.

"Well, what's it going to be, Lisha?"

Jalisha walked toward the top landing of the stairs and took a seat on the top step. She rested her chin on top of her knees and thought back to her dream of Corine. "Please don't end up used up and no good to anyone like Camille." Corine's words taunted her mind. Tears welled in her eyes because she was afraid of going at it alone. She started sobbing uncontrollably.

"Baby, what's wrong?"

"I'm scared, Derek. Suppose I can't do it? Suppose I can't survive without turning tricks?"

"Baby, there is nothing to be afraid of. I will be by your side."

She looked up and gazed at him with her bloodshot eyes.

Derek palmed her face and used his thumbs to wipe away her tears.

"Do you promise?" she asked.

"Yes, sweetheart, I promise. You'll be okay. I have faith in you, Jalisha."

Jalisha threw her arms around Derek's neck. "Other than Corine, no one has ever said those words to me before."

Derek kissed Jalisha on her forehead, pulled her to her feet, and led her to the bedroom.

# Chapter 34

The next day, Jalisha sat with her legs crossed Indian style in the middle of her bed. Before her was the Sunday's employment section of The Washington Post. As she perused the help wanted ads, she feasted on her favorite snack of Nacho Cheese Doritos and Vanilla Pepsi. She used a red pen and crossed through the ads requiring qualifications she did not possess and circled those requiring no experience. Some of the ads even required a college degree. She wished…maybe one day she would be able to get her GED and then go to college. Now all she needed was a resume. She hadn't a clue as to what a resume even looked like. She couldn't recall ever seeing one before. It didn't make sense to her that The Washington Post didn't give clues as to what the hell a resume was. All the ads said was, "Please submit resumes to…"

What the fuck is a damn resume?

As she pondered on how she was going to get her hands on a resume, she was startled by the loud outburst of the ringing telephone. As she reached for the phone, her bag of Doritos fell over and chips spilled onto her brand new duvet. After frolicking on Derek's duvet, she had decided to stop by JC Penney's on the way home.

"Shit!" she exclaimed. She nestled the phone

between her chin and shoulders while she picked up the chips. "Hello?"

"Hi, baby." Derek's deep baritone voice always sent chills throughout her.

"Hey, sweetie. What's going on?"

"Not much, just missing you."

"Aw, how sweet. I miss you too."

She could hear Derek's smile through the phone when he said, "Yeah, whatever."

"So, what do I owe the pleasure?"

"Calling to see what you're up to?"

"Well, I'm looking through the employment section of the newspaper."

"Really?" he asked excitedly. "Baby, I'm so proud of you!"

"Yeah, well, don't go getting excited. I don't have a job yet."

"But you will. I have faith in you, babe."

"I don't know, Derek. By the way, what the fuck is a resume?"

"Oh, well, a resume is a listing of all of your qualifications and prior job experience."

"Well, that shuts me out. All of these ads want a resume. No point in sending in a resume if I don't have any qualifications or jobs to list."

"Hmmm…well, babe, don't go getting discouraged."

Jalisha took a deep sigh of defeat and frustration.

"Babe, how're you looking on funds?"

"What do you mean?"

"Until you find a job, you'll need money. Do you have any?"

"Oh yeah, I'm cool in that department. I learned how to stash away money from Camille. I have enough to last me for a good six months."

"Good. You know I'm here if you need anything, right?"

"Right," she smiled. "Hey, I'm hungry. You hungry?"

"Come to think of it...yeah, I'm hungry and I want to see a movie too."

"Oh baby, can we please go see Barbershop? Please!"

Derek chuckled and replied, "Pick you up in an hour."

"Okey-dokey," she giggled and hung up the phone.

She closed the bag of Doritos, swallowed the remainder of the Vanilla Pepsi, and hopped off the bed. She opened her closet door and stood before the hundreds of dollars worth of clothing she had managed to purchase during her years of prostitution. Then, it dawned on her that she might never be able to shop again, working a regular job.

"Oh well, all in the name of love," she muttered.

From the closet, she retrieved her Apple Bottom jeans with the button down fly and a pink baby doll top with the letter J inscribed over her left breast. From the shoe bag hanging on the back of her closet door, she pulled out her black leather cowboy boots. She reached high above the closet to retrieve her black leather cowboy hat. She was all set for Derek...if she was going to a rodeo, that is. Jalisha had a style like no other. She was truly her own individual woman.

After she showered and dressed, she stood before

the floor-length mirror in the hallway and admired herself.

"Well, at least Camille did something right."

She smiled at her reflection and headed for the sofa. She reached for *The Coldest Winter Ever*, and picked up where she had left off, at chapter ten, while she waited for Derek.

# *Chapter 35*

After dining at the Silver Diner, Derek and Jalisha caught the one o'clock showing of Barbershop at Hoffman Theaters in Alexandria, Virginia. For it to be a holiday, the theater was pretty quiet, with the exception of Derek, Jalisha, and the five other people who were, probably for the first time, enjoying the movie without anyone talking back to the screen or on a cellular phone.

Derek and Jalisha took seats on the empty third row from the top. Before the movie could start good, Derek had Jalisha on her back with her legs dangled over the back of the seats in front of them. Fortunately, for her, the armrests were in the upright position.

"Derek, we can't do this," she whispered. "I ain't having sex in here, boy."

"Shh, before they hear you. We're not going to have sex, just having a little fun."

Derek covered Jalisha's lips with his and unbuttoned her jeans.

"Derek, cut it out. I want to watch the movie."

The movie was at the part where Ice Cube was telling Eve to stop cussin' when Derek's hand slithered down Jalisha's jeans and into her panties. His finger flicked away at her clitoris, causing her hips to move and her juices to flow.

Jalisha grabbed hold of Derek's behind and pulled him into her. Her desire for him was at an all time high.

Something about sneaking sex really excited her. She looked forward to many more escapades such as this with Derek.

"Baby, stick it in me."

"Here?" he asked, as if he were chickening out.

"Yes," she panted. "You can't be getting me all excited and not do anything about it. Besides, can't nobody see us. There's nobody up here but us anyway."

Derek popped up his head and looked around. At that moment, not a soul was around and the closest movie watchers were at least twenty rows below them.

"Come on, Derek." Her pants were heavier and deeper.

Derek unzipped his pants and released the head of his dick.

"Pull your pants down, baby."

Derek pulled himself off Jalisha, looked around once again, and slid down in his seat. He pulled his pants down around his ankles. Then, he turned toward Jalisha and pulled her jeans down around her ankles, pulling one leg out.

Jalisha tossed her unconfined leg over the row in from of them, while the other leg was stretched out before Derek.

Derek positioned himself on top of Jalisha and fingered her one more time before inserting his gardening tool into her secret garden. Well, her garden really wasn't a secret, seeing as though half of Metropolitan's finest as well as many other strays knew all about her garden.

# AppleTree

Derek climaxed when Ice Cube bailed Michael Ealy out of jail. Needless to say, Jalisha had missed the movie.

# *Chapter 36*

"I need a resume," Jalisha said. "Will you help me write one?"

Derek thumbed the steering wheel to the beat of The Temptation's I Want a Love.

"Why do you listen to old music?"

"Baby, they don't make music like that anymore. That kind of music is good for the soul."

"Uh huh, now what about my resume, Derek?"

"I'll give you a copy of mine and you can use that to go by."

"Fine," she pouted.

She didn't need him to give her a copy of his resume. What she really wanted was for him to write up her resume for her.

After Derek dropped her off, Jalisha moped into her apartment, pulled out a paper and pencil from the kitchen drawer, and set out to write her resume. She took a deep sigh and looked toward the bookshelf. There had to be something on the shelf to help her with her resume. She thumbed through the bookshelf...nothing.

Three hours later, she had completed her resume. Whether it was in the right format, she didn't know. It was handwritten. She figured she had to type it up, but she didn't own a typewriter or a computer. She never had the need for one. However, she would go to Kinko's tomorrow and use the computers to type up her resume. She placed her resume on the coffee table, leaned back onto the sofa, and flashed a smile of completion.

She tucked her legs beneath her and decided to call Derek on his cellular phone. "Baby, guess what?"

"What, sweetness?"

"I finished my resume!"

"Well all right now, babe! That's wonderful. I'm very proud of you, Lisha."

"Thank you!"

"Read it to me."

"Huh?"

"I want to hear what you have."

"No," she snapped.

"Why not?"

"Because…"

"Lisha, come on. I might be able to help you with it."

"All right," she replied reluctantly.

She reached for her resume and cleared her throat.

"Well, I put my name and address, of course."

"Of course…"

"Then, following the outline of your resume, I wrote down an objective."

"Okay, let me hear it."

"I will, dang, give me a chance."

Derek chuckled. "Okay, I'll shut up and listen."

"Thank you," she said sarcastically.

"Anyway, for my objective, I wrote: To obtain a position with an organization allowing career growth." She hesitated, waiting for his approval.

Derek was quiet.

"Then," she continued, "you had education. Well, I don't have any education, so…um, I lied and wrote down that I am a high school graduate with a few college credits." She hesitated again, waiting for his approval.

Derek was quiet.

"Derek? Aren't you going to say anything?"

"You told me to be quiet," he chuckled.

"See?"

"Baby, it all sounds good so far. But, where did you attend college?" He laughed.

"Fuck you, Derek. never mind."

"No, no, no. I'm sorry. Um, put down you took classes at the University of District of Columbia."

"Okay," she said, jotting down on her resume. "What else?"

"Um, well, what type of classes did you take?"

"Well…I dunno. Do I have to put that down?"

"Yes. They are going to want to know what classes you took, to see if you would enhance the position."

"Well shoot, I don't know nothing about what kind of courses they have in college."

"Okay, write down Business Management."

"What? Business Management?"

"Yes. You have business management skills."

"No, I don't!"

"Yes, you do, Lisha. You've been managing your own business for years. Although it's a business you can't reference on a resume, it was a business just the same."

"Are you trying to be funny, Derek?"

"No," he answered, laughing hysterically.

# Apple Tree

Jalisha got so mad at Derek she slammed the phone down. "I'll do it my damn self!"

## *Chapter 37*

Monday morning, Jalisha got up bright and early. She showered, scrambled eggs, fried bacon, and camped out in front of the telephone. The employment section sat before her, covered in X and O's and resembling a game of tic-tac-toe. She was determined to get a job. She didn't know whom to call first, so she closed her eyes and played One Potato, Two Potato, Three Potato, Four. Her finger landed on Radix II, an organization supplying computer systems to the District and Federal governments. She dialed the number and held her breath.

"Radix II, how may I direct your call?"

She quickly looked at the ad. A contact person was not listed.

"Yes, may I help you please?"

"Oh…yes, my name is Jalisha Thomas. I'm calling about your ad in The Washington Post for a receptionist?"

"Sure, I'll connect you to Holly Hunt. One moment please."

Jalisha took several quick, deep breaths and tried to maintain her composure.

"Holly Hunt."

"Yes, Ms. Hunt, my name is Jalisha Thomas. I am calling about your employment ad for a receptionist."

"Have you any experience at being a receptionist?"

"No, Ma'am. Your ad says, 'No experience necessary.'"

"Yes it does, doesn't it? The salary is quite low, starting at $15,000 per year."

Jalisha's mouth fell open. Fifteen thousand dollars a year? What the fuck?

"Of course, you'll have full benefits with 401K and free parking."

"Thank you, Ms. Hunt, but I'm no longer interested in your position."

"Ms. Thomas, for someone with no experience, $15,000 is the going rate."

"That may be so. However, I'll have to decline."

"Well, Ms. Thomas, you can't decline an offer that has not been extended."

Jalisha mumbled, "Whatever," and then hung up the phone.

She decided not to repeat the One Potato, Two Potato and would simply start calling from the top until she received a positive response. She had something to prove, but they could kiss her ass with that $15,000 shit. She thought an offering so little had to be against the law.

She picked up the receiver and dialed again.

"Good morning, Barlow & Associates."

"Good morning. My name is Jalisha Thomas and I'm calling about your ad in The Washington Post for a receptionist."

"I'll connect you with personnel. One moment."

While she waited, Jalisha tapped her pen on the table to calm her nerves. This shit is for the birds, she thought. No wonder Camille never thought twice about a real job…$15,000 indeed.

"Personnel, Verna speaking."

"Good morning, Verna. My name is Jalisha Thomas. I'm calling about the receptionist position."

"Do you have any experience?"

Jalisha took a silent sigh. Here we go again with this shit.

"No. I don't have any experience. However, I do answer the phone at home."

Verna chuckled and said, "That was cute."

"Thank you."

"Okay, Ms. Thomas, I'll tell you what. I placed that ad three weeks ago and you are the first person to inquire. I guess receptionist positions are below folks these days."

"Uh, if you don't mind me asking, what's the salary?"

"Don't mind at all. The beginning salary is $25,500 plus a full benefits package. I don't know how many companies you've contacted so far, but our salary scale is very competitive."

Jalisha started to get excited. "Ms. Verna…"

"Verna is fine, honey. I'm not that old," she said as they both chuckled.

"Verna, is there room for advancement?" She remembered Derek had insisted she ask that question. He told her there was no point in taking a dead end job.

"Absolutely. As a matter of fact, we encourage it. We'd rather fill positions from within. We provide training and we also offer tuition reimbursement."

"Tuition reimbursement?"

"Um hum, if you want to take college courses, we'll reimburse eighty percent of the tuition. However, you must maintain a B average."

"I'll take the job!" she yelled with excitement.

Verna was tickled at Jalisha's enthusiasm. She liked Jalisha from the start.

"Hold on, sweetie. Before I can offer you the position, we have to follow protocol. I'll need you to fax me your resume. Then I will need you to come in for an interview. If things go well, we'll extend you an offer. How's that?"

Jalisha hesitated. She thought about her resume, filled with all lies. Would Verna be able to see through the lies on a piece of paper? "Verna, I don't have any experience as a receptionist."

"I figured as much, honey. It's all right though. We'll train you on our phone system. It's an old system. We usually have to train everyone we hire."

"I'm a quick learner."

"How about you come in for an interview tomorrow at two o'clock? You can bring me your resume then."

"Okay, that'll be fine."

"Great! I look forward to meeting you tomorrow, Jalisa."

"It's Jalisha."

"Yes, Jalisha. See you tomorrow."

# Chapter 38

That evening, Derek was due at her place for dinner. At that time, she would share the news about her interview tomorrow with Verna. She was so excited she didn't know what to do. Most importantly, she was excited she would still be able to shop!

She prepared Derek's favorite meal of Sloppy Joes, French fries, and vanilla milkshakes. When he arrived, she greeted him with a tight hug and a suffocating kiss on the lips.

"What was that for?" he asked, a smile stretching across his face.

"I've got good news!"

"Hmm, I smell Sloppy Joes. Can you tell me the good news over dinner? I'm starved, babe."

Derek followed Jalisha into the kitchen. She pulled out a potato roll and spooned on a mound of Sloppy Joe.

"You want some cheese?" she asked.

Derek nodded his head yes. "So, what's the news?" he asked, enjoying his Sloppy Joe.

"I have a job interview tomorrow."

"Hey, that's wonderful, Lisha. See? I told you things would work out."

"I'm so excited. It's a receptionist position though."

"And? Honey, the receptionist is an integral part of

the organization. Someone has to greet and transfer calls from the clients."

"Really? Well, I don't know what to wear."

"Be very professional. No jeans, tank tops, nothing like that. Wear a dress or business suit."

Jalisha twisted up her lips in thought. "I don't think I own a business suit."

"Well, it doesn't have to be a business suit, so long as you're professional looking."

"I think I can pull it off."

"I'm sure you can. I've seen your closet," he teased.

"Oh, shut up," she chuckled. "How's your Sloppy Joe?"

"The bomb!"

He leaned in and kissed her on the cheek.

"What was that for?"

"Just because."

Jalisha grabbed her plate and went into the living room. She sat her plate on the coffee table and walked toward the entertainment center. She searched for her all time favorite movie, The Color Purple, and slid it into the VCR.

Derek sat on the sofa and crossed one leg over the other. "Not Ms. Celie again!"

"Don't be knocking my girl, Celie. I keep watching in hopes she will slit Mister's throat."

"Well, after watching it for the hundredth time, if she hasn't slit his throat by now, she ain't gonna."

"Uh huh, and that's only 'cause Shug got to her before she slid that razor across his throat."

"Yeah and she would've 'sat in that jail' like Sophia, 'cause she be a big woman."

"You know what, Derek?" she laughed. "You have issues."

"I have issues?" Derek reached out for Jalisha. "Come here, woman!"

Jalisha reached out for his hand and sat down beside him.

"Have I told you how proud I am of you?"

"Yes, you have, Derek."

"Good, because I'm so proud of you."

"Thank you, baby," she said, leaning in close to his face. They rubbed noses.

Derek leaned back and admired Jalisha's beauty.

"What?" she asked.

"Do you want to have children?"

"I don't know. I've never thought much about it. Do you?"

"Eventually."

"Why you asking about babies? Are you pregnant?" She chuckled.

Derek playfully popped Jalisha upside the head. "No, silly, I'd like to get married and have children. I want a family. You know what I mean?"

"Yeah, I know. I don't know if I'd be a good mother though. After all, I didn't have a very good role model," she pouted. She used the remote to start the movie.

"Camille wasn't all that bad..."

Jalisha cut him short with a look of 'are you crazy or something?'

"Okay, turning your daughter out to do tricks isn't cool, but she did what she knew."

Jalisha grunted and adjusted herself beneath his underarm.

"Lisha, did you know your grandmother?"

"Naw, she died before Corey and I were born and Camille never spoke of her."

"What about your grandfather?"

"Same thing."

"Wow. That must've been tough, not knowing your grandparents."

"Not really. I mean you can't miss something or someone you never had, right?"

"Right, right."

"D, I wish my life could've been different, but it wasn't. I craved to have my mother love me, but she didn't. I craved a normal childhood, but I never had it. So, if I ever have children, I do know they will have everything I never had."

"Which is?"

"A normal life outside of the projects, with a mother and father who love them unconditionally."

Derek kissed Jalisha on the forehead and then stroked her hair.

"If I can give you what you want, Lisha, I will. You have my word on that one."

Jalisha gazed up at her man. She wondered what she did to deserve such a good man. She thanked God daily for Derek.

Derek tasted her lips and leaned back against the sofa as Jalisha stretched out on top of him. They watched as Celie and Nettie frolicked through the field of purple.

# *Chapter 39*

The next morning, Jalisha rose early to prepare for her very first interview. She was nervous as hell and Derek was kind enough to type up her resume and cover letter. She was all set. All she needed was business attire. She flung open her closet door and scanned the merchandise. Everything she owned was either denim-related, had a crotch-high split, or was halter-tops.

She checked the digital clock on the nightstand. Her interview was at two o'clock and she had a few hours to spare. She slipped into her jeans, tee shirt, and Nike running shoes and headed to Farragut West Metro station. Her next stop, Pentagon City.

She dashed through Macy's and grabbed the first business-like suit she saw. Now, she needed shoes. All of her shoes were either flats or stilettos, and she was sure Verna wouldn't appreciate a prospective employee showing up in stiletto heels. She stopped in the shoe department and bought a basic black pump. It wasn't quite her style, but it looked professional.

If I get this job, I'll have to get a new wardrobe, she thought aloud. Derek was definitely going to pay for a new wardrobe since this is what he wanted.

Still, she had to be honest with herself. She wanted this change of event in her life more than Derek did. She always wanted to get out of the profession, but she didn't know how. She needed that special push and

# Apple Tree

Derek was the one to administer it. For the first time in her life, she knew what it felt like to be blessed with a gift, a gift of friendship and love.

On her way home, she decided to stop at the Hallmark store on K Street. She spent thirty minutes searching for the perfect card for Derek, which would express exactly how she felt about him. Although every card she came across was fitting, they weren't fitting enough. Therefore, she purchased a blank card with a picture of two lovebirds on the cover and a soft, cuddly, white teddy bear with a tag around its neck that read, "I Love You Truly."

As she walked home, she was in deep thought trying to figure out exactly what she would write on the inside of the card. She knew how she felt about Derek, but she wasn't very good at penning her thoughts on paper. Even though she read O Magazine monthly, where Oprah often talked about journaling your thoughts, she never could quite grasp the technique. Besides, she never really had any feelings until Derek.

It was noon when she returned home. She took a shower, applied a light coverage of her favorite make-up, Mac, and wrapped her hair up in a scarf. Her outfit, consisting of a black silk pantsuit, a red shell, black pantyhose, and the basic black pump, lay sprawled across her bed. She had an hour to spare. She was fortunate to find a position that was in walking distance from her apartment.

She retrieved the Hallmark bag from the living room and returned to her bedroom, where she sat on the edge of bed gazing at the card. She picked up a pen and not having a clue as to what she was going to write, she began with:

*Dear Derek,*

*I'm not good at jotting down my thoughts or feelings, but I felt it was something I needed to do. I wanted to give you a token of my appreciation. I wanted to let you know how much you've changed my life. I want you to know my feelings for you are strong. I want you to know I love you. Thank you for accepting me and allowing me to be me.*

*All my love,*

*Lisha*

She read what she wrote with satisfaction. She inserted the card into the matching envelope, licked the flap, and sealed the envelope. On the front of the envelope, she wrote, "To Derek." She sat the teddy bear on the nightstand and propped the card against the teddy bear. She marveled at the thought of Derek's expression once he read the card.

The digital clock read one o'clock. Jalisha stood to her feet, took a deep sigh, and proceeded to dress herself. When she looked into the full-length mirror, she didn't recognize the image before her.

"Oh my God!" she exclaimed. "Is that really me?"

She couldn't believe her eyes. She looked damn good. She finger combed her hair, turned around a few times, grabbed her purse, coat, and resume, and was out the door.

# Chapter 40

Barlow & Associates was located on the tenth floor of One Thomas Circle, NW. Jalisha stood nervously in the lobby and waited for the elevator to descend. She wiggled her toes in her new shoes. Her toes felt cramped. She wasn't use to wearing closed toe shoes. When the elevator doors opened, she hesitated and, under her breath, recited the Lord's Prayer…what little of it she knew. As Jalisha stepped onto the elevator, a slew of people bombarded her and crowded the elevator. She was squished in the back. She began to panick. There were entirely too many people jammed in there for her liking.

When the elevator ascended to the tenth floor, Jalisha pushed her way from the back and out into the lobby of Barlow & Associates. Small designer chairs flanked each side of the lobby. In the center of the lobby, there stood a glass table with a huge multi-color floral arrangement situated in the middle. The specially made area rug coordinated with the floral arrangement.

"Good afternoon. May I help you?" asked the elderly woman seated behind the concierge desk.

"Hello. I have an appointment with Verna." Jalisha felt so unprofessional because she didn't know Verna's last name.

"And your name?"

"Jalisha Thomas."

"All right, Ms. Thomas, have a seat and I'll let Ms. Jones know you are here."

Jalisha made a mental note of Verna's last name.

Since Verna was on CP time, Jalisha decided to thumb through the various legal publications that sat on the table beside her. She hadn't a clue what the hell she was reading, but she did get a clue she must be at a law firm.

A plump lady with a very attractive face graced the lobby with her presence. Ringlets of her hair softly framed her latte face as it flowed down her back. Jalisha wondered if Verna's hair was a weave because it was excessively thick for it to be natural.

"Jalisha?"

Jalisha stood to her feet and smiled.

Verna extended her hand and Jalisha gracefully accepted it. "It's nice to finally meet you."

"Likewise," she answered, clearing the frog from her throat.

"Did you bring your resume?"

"Yes." Jalisha reached into her leather satchel and retrieved the envelope addressed to Verna, Barlow & Associates. "My apologies for not including your last name. I didn't know it until now."

"That's quite all right. Now, this shouldn't take long. I have two people I'd like you to speak with. For the most part, our decision has been made. We are going to extend you an offer if all goes well with the interviews."

Excitement shot through Jalisha. She tried to abstain from bursting into glorious laughter.

Verna noticed her excitement and chuckled. She took to Jalisha immediately.

"Let's get started."

Jalisha followed on Verna's heels and a look of amazement never left her face. This was the first professional office she'd visited. She felt like a kid in a candy store and knew she was going to enjoy working there. Her life was looking up, and she was beginning to feel better about herself.

Two hours later, Verna shook Jalisha's hand and said, "Welcome to Barlow & Associates."

Jalisha was speechless.

"Your reference checked out."

References, she thought. What the hell is she talking about?

"Mr. McDuffie spoke highly of you."

Mr. McDuffie?

"He said he was sorry to see you go, but wished nothing but the best for you."

Huh? Then it finally dawned on her. That damn Derek, she chuckled to herself.

"We're so happy to have you join us," she smiled. "As we discussed yesterday, the starting salary is $25,500 with a full benefits package. We are a small law firm. You will be the main receptionist with backup from the administrative assistants, as needed. Vestina's last day is next week. Mr. McDuffie will allow you to come in for training later in the week."

"How nice of him," she commented, displaying a broad smile. What am I going to do with that fool?

"I will send you an offer letter with all of the specifics for your new position. I'll need you to sign it and return to me as soon as possible. I'd like you to start in two weeks. Is that okay?"

"Yes, that's fine."

Jalisha felt suffocated. She wanted to scream, she was so elated. She wanted to get out of there so she could jump for joy.

"Well, unless you have questions, I'll see you on Thursday at eight-thirty for a two-hour training session."

"All right, I'll see you then. Thank you so much, Ms. Jones."

"Call me Verna, and you're welcome."

# *Chapter 41*

That evening, Jalisha glared at the card she had intended to give to Derek and thought it wasn't enough to show her appreciation for all he'd done for her. After all, this wasn't the first time Derek was there for her. She remembered back to the night Corine bashed Camille upside the head with a porcelain doll, killing her. When she didn't know whom or where to turn, she called Derek and he was like Johnny on the spot.

Although Jalisha wasn't a churchgoer, she knew about God and having faith. She didn't pray all of the time, but when she did, it made her feel good. As she never attended church, she did watch Pastor Fred Price every Sunday morning at eight o'clock. A long time ago, when Camille turned her out, she prayed to God for the first time. She prayed for someone to come into her life and rescue her and Corine. She didn't realize it then, but God had sent Derek. And He had sent him again. This time, she wouldn't let this blessing from God go unappreciated.

She racked her brain trying to think of ways she could show her gratitude to Derek. Derek is a simple man. He doesn't want for anything and has everything he needs…except for a family, she thought. Without a second thought, she slipped into her jeans and a top and headed for the CVS on Thomas Circle.

"Excuse me, where are your ovulation kits?" she asked the clerk behind the register.

"Aisle nine," the clerk responded with a smile.

"Thank you," she chirped.

Jalisha moseyed down aisle nine and immediately grabbed a First Response Ovulation Kit. "Damn, $14.99!" she said to no one in particular. "Oh well," she sighed, "he's worth it."

Back at home, she sat on the edge of the bathtub and read and re-read the instructions. According to the directions, she was at her peak and would wait until morning to take the test. Actually, she always knew when she was ovulating. She could feel it and, not to mention, the white mucus she discharged seven days before her cycle. She placed the kit on the sink and left it for the night.

Jalisha sat on the edge of her bed and felt solemn. This was one of those times she wished she had a friend. She wished she had Corine to talk with. She had no one to share her innermost feelings, her pains, or her joys with. At that moment, she felt lonely.

Before bed, she dropped down to her knees, clasped her hands together, and said a prayer.

"Dear God, thank you for all of the blessings you've given me. Thank you for Derek. I don't know what I would do without him. Most importantly, though, thank you for letting Corine come to me in my dream. God, I don't want to be selfish, but do you think you could allow her to come to my dreams again? I miss her so much and I really need to talk to her. Thank you, God. Oh and by the way, if you see Camille, could you please tell her I said hello and I forgive her for everything? Amen."

Jalisha climbed into bed, pulled the covers under her chin, and went fast to sleep.

# *Chapter 42*

"See, Lisha, God does answer prayers." Like an angel, Corine stood over Jalisha, her halo shining bright as the North Star. "Hello, Jalisha."

"Corey?"

"It's me. I can't stay long, though, so let's get down to business. What's troubling you, Lisha?"

Jalisha leaned up on her elbows and adjusted her vision.

"I've been watching you, Lisha. I'm so glad you've decided to change your life."

"Yes, he is something, isn't he?"

"Yes, he certainly is."

"Have you seen Camille yet?"

"No, not yet."

"Oh," Jalisha replied, feeling awfully sad.

Jalisha never wished any harm to come to Camille, but she didn't want to think of her spending the rest of eternity in hell either.

"Corey, I miss you something awful. I have no friends, no one to talk with."

"You have Derek."

"I know…"

"And soon you'll be starting a new job…"

"How did you know about that?"

Corine looked up toward the ceiling and smiled.

"Hopefully, I'll make friends on the job, but you

know I don't trust a soul, which is probably why I don't have any friends. I don't have time for drama and all the mess that comes with having girlfriends."

"Jalisha, open your heart. God will not send you dysfunctional people. He will fill your life with wonderful people. Granted, some of those people may end up being trying obstacles, but those obstacles will make you stronger."

Jalisha looked up at Corine and smiled.

"Well, I have to go, Lisha."

"Will I see you again, Corey?"

"Keep praying and I'll always be here."

"I love you, Corey. Take care of yourself."

"Oh, I'm fine, big sister. You can trust that. You take care of yourself. Lisha, continue to be true to you and all will work out  fine. Derek loves you. Love him back."

Just as she appeared, Corine was gone.

Jalisha's throat felt strained from stifling the tears. She sat up in the bed and cried like a baby. She then wiped away her tears with the back of her hand and jumped out of bed. She dropped to her knees and said a prayer.

"Dear God, thank you for allowing Corey to visit me. If there's anything I can do for you, don't hesitate to ask. Amen."

With a light heart and a smile on her face, she hopped into bed. The Sandman gently rocked her back to sleep.

## *Chapter 43*

Thursday morning, Jalisha entered Barlow & Associates, ready to start her new life. The night before, Derek treated her to a shopping spree at her favorite department store, Macy's.

She was eager to start work and they were eager as well. When she stepped off the elevator, Verna greeted her.

"Jalisha, we are so excited you have joined us. You'll definitely enjoy your stay."

Jalisha smiled and nodded her head in agreement.

"First things first, let's get to know the office."

Jalisha followed on Verna's heels. The first stop was the coat closet.

"This is where everyone hangs their coat. We'd prefer you not to hang your coat at the workstation. The partners like to keep the office looking uniformed and clutter-free."

Jalisha nodded her understanding of the rules and continued on Verna's heels, like an abandoned child touring her new home at an orphanage.

Verna introduced Jalisha to several people, all of whom she will never remember. When they approached the last office, they stood at the door and waited for approval to enter the office.

The man had his back turned toward Jalisha and Verna, while he discussed business over the phone. He was tall, extremely handsome and the color of latte lick. With curly hair, hazel eyes and a muscular build, Jalisha felt like she knew him.

"No problem. I'll have my assistant draw up the papers and courier them over to your office for your signature." As he turned around to face his 'ladies in waiting,' he flashed a Colgate smile and Jalisha nearly dropped to her knees.

Jalisha gasped and covered her mouth.

"Are you all right?" Verna asked.

Jalisha gathered her bearings and nodded yes.

"All right, will do. I'll look forward to hearing from you," the latte lick man said as he hung up the phone.

"Good morning, Alfred. Sorry to disturb you. I wanted you to meet our new receptionist," she smiled, turning toward Jalisha.

"Jalisha Thomas, meet Alfred Malloy. Alfred is also a partner."

Jalisha's mouth was open, but not a word could she speak. She was looking at a reflection of herself.

Alfred squared his shoulders and maintained a stern face. He extended his hand toward Jalisha. "Welcome to Barlow & Associates, Jalisha. I'm sure you'll enjoy working here."

Jalisha was at a loss for words.

Verna stared at her like she was crazy and whispered, "Jalisha? Aren't you going to say something?"

"Uh…uh, good morning," she managed. Her throat was dry as the desert and felt like sandpaper when she tried to speak. "Excuse me," she said and darted out the office, down the hall, and into the ladies room.

Jalisha stood over the sink trying to catch her breath.

She felt a possible hyperventilation coming on. She turned on the cold-water faucet and splashed water on her face several times. When she looked into the mirror, she didn't see Jalisha. She saw a raccoon. Her mascara had bled down her cheeks and onto the lapel of her mustard-colored, silk blouse. She reached for a paper towel, dabbed it in the stream of cold water, and blotted the black smudge from her lapel.

"I don't believe this shit," she mouthed. "It can't be," she muttered. "Of all places...it can't be!"

She placed her hands to her face and wept uncontrollably.

Verna barged into the ladies room and stared her down. "What is wrong with you? Are you all right?"

"Yes, I'm fine," she mustered. "I feel a little sick."

"Well, I hope you're coming down with a cold and nothing more serious. I'd hate to have to hire a temp for a receptionist who has yet to start the job," she chuckled.

"I'll be fine. I need a minute, if you don't mind."

"Sure. Once you get yourself together, Mr. Malloy asked to have a chat with you."

"Why?" she gasped.

Verna looked at her puzzled. "I don't know. I suppose he wants to make sure you're all right. After all, you ran out of his office as if you'd seen a ghost."

"I don't want to talk to him, Verna," she pleaded.

"He doesn't bite, Jalisha."

"I'm afraid...um, he may fire me or something."

"Why on earth would he fire you? Oh, you're being silly, girl," Verna said, brushing off Jalisha fears. "Now, get yourself together and go see what he wants.

Afterward, come to my office and we'll start the training. All right?"

Jalisha nodded with the look of desperation in her eyes.

"Good," Verna said and rested her hand on Jalisha's shoulder. "I'll see you in a bit."

Jalisha wiped the bleeding mascara from her face, finger combed her hair, and smoothed her hand over her blouse and down to her waist, where she adjusted her slacks. She knew one day she would have to face the man she only knew as her deadbeat daddy. However, she wanted it to be on her terms.

Jalisha gently tapped on Alfred's door. "You wanted to see me," she said softly, her words barely audible.

"Yes, I did." He motioned toward the chair positioned in front of his desk. "Have a seat."

"No, thank you. I'll stand."

"All right, if you insist."

"I do," she said sternly.

Jalisha was determined to stand her ground. There was nothing he could say to erase all of the years of feeling her father didn't want anything to do with her or Corine.

Alfred stood by the window and glared out at the traffic rushing around Thomas Circle. "Everyone is in such a hurry to go nowhere," he said, not knowing what to say to the daughter who he hadn't seen since she was two years old.

Jalisha inhaled deeply and asked, "Why?"

"Why what?" he replied, his back facing her.

"Why did you leave us?"

"I didn't leave you…"

"Yes, you did!"

"Look, you were too young to understand."

"Mama said you didn't want to have anything to do with us."

"That's not true, Lisha."

"Jalisha," she snapped between clinched teeth. "My name is Jalisha. Only select people can call me Lisha."

He felt the poison of the Black Widow flow slowly through his veins.

He took a sigh of defeat. "Jalisha, so many times I've tried to see you and Camille wouldn't allow it. She said you didn't want to be bothered with me."

"You're lying," she spewed.

He shook his head profusely. "Camille forbade me to see you. She took me to court for child support every single year since you were three years old. Yet, I could never see you. Hell, I didn't even know where you lived."

Jalisha narrowed her eyes at Alfred. "Why do you keep saying me? What about Corine?"

He turned his back to her and stared blankly out the window. "Corine was not my daughter."

Jalisha stared at him in disbelief. Tears welled in her eyes.

He faced her. "I thought you knew," he said in a consoling voice.

"I don't understand. Camille said you were our father and you divorced her after Corey was born."

He shook his head. "Not so. First of all, I was never married to Camille. She left me for Corine's father."

Jalisha felt weak in the knees. She felt like she was going to lose it. Shakily, she slowly walked toward the mocha brown leather sofa and took a seat. She felt lightheaded, almost ready to pass out.

"Are you all right?" Alfred asked.

She looked past him and asked, "That day I called you and told you about Corine...the day after she died, you weren't nice at all. You said she deserved whatever happened to her. You said that because she wasn't your daughter?"

"I said that because I felt bitterness for all those years of having to the deal with knowing the woman I loved more than anything in this world was a prostitute and was pregnant by one of her johns. That john was Corine's father, Jalisha." He sat down on the sofa beside her. He felt himself becoming lightheaded and was desperately in need of air. "Before Corine was born, your mother had me to believe she was my child. After she was born, and several months went by, I was hearing talk around town about Camille prostituting and how much of a fool I was to be with her. I had no idea..." He trailed off into deep thought, his voice shaky. "When I insisted on a paternity test, Camille left me."

Jalisha shook her head and cried all at the same time. "I don't know what to say. All of these years, I thought you had deserted us."

"I would've never done that, sweetheart. You have to believe that."

Jalisha didn't know what to believe. She knew Camille was capable of many things, but keeping her father away from her was so hard for her to swallow.

"I always wanted a relationship with you. I tried many times to find you, but each time I did, Camille would move. After awhile, I gave up. I had hoped when you became old enough, and if you wanted to see me, you would try and find me."

"This is all too much for me," she cried, her eyes bloodshot red.

"Now that we've reunited, I'd like to get to know you, my daughter."

Jalisha stared into space. At that moment, the only one she could think about was Derek. He had become her security blanket, the one to cling to when things didn't seem to go right.

"I'll have to think about it," she said, unsure if this was what she really wanted. "I'm supposed to be in Verna's office by now. I don't want to get into any trouble."

"You won't get into any trouble. I'm the one who hired you."

Alfred's confession confused her. "What do you mean? I thought Verna hired me."

He unintentionally chuckled at her ignorance. "Well, she extended the offer. However, she had to pass it by the partners…and I am a partner." He smiled warmly.

"So you knew…"

He nodded his head, with the smile still in place.

"This is way too much for me right now," she uttered.

"Take the day off. Start tomorrow instead. I'll let Verna know."

"Really? Are you sure?"

"I'm sure," he said, this time with a smile that showed his happiness of being reunited with his daughter. Unfortunately, she was a grown woman now. He missed out on so many years. Would he be able to get them back? Would Jalisha give him the opportunity to make up for lost time?

## *Chapter 44*

Jalisha's head throbbed to the tenth degree. She popped Tylenol and Advil and there still was no relief in sight. She slithered into bed, pulled the covers beneath her chin, and closed her eyes. The thoughts of earlier events caused her head to pound more.

"Stop it," she whispered. "Please stop."

Thoughts of Camille tap-danced in her mind…rat-a-tat-tat was all she heard for the next hour until she fell off to sleep.

Her lovely vision leaned on the pillow and began stroking hair away from Jalisha's brow.

Jalisha restlessly tossed and turned unaware of Corine's angelic presence.

"Lisha?" Corine whispered in her ear. "Hey sis," she said, kissing her on the cheek.

Jalisha slowly opened her eyes and smiled. "Hey, Corey."

"How are you, Lisha?"

"I'm fine. It's good to see you again."

"It's good to see you too, sis. I can't stay long, so I'll get to the point."

Jalisha pulled herself up on her elbows and squinted, adjusting her vision. "All right," she said while nodding.

"You saw Daddy today."

"How do you know that?"

Corine smiled and said, "I told you I'm always with you."

"Yeah, I saw him today. Can't say I was elated though."

"I'm sure, but it's all Camille's fault."

"So, if you were there, then you know he's not your father."

"Yes, I know." Her expression was sad and sullen-like. "It's okay though. I had you and you were all I needed." She smiled her angelic smile. "However, he is your father, and you should mend things with him."

"I don't know, Corey. He can't come back into my life after all of these years."

"It wasn't his fault he wasn't in your life. It was Camille's. She is the one who kept your father away from you. She is the one who deprived you of having a father. Now he's back in your life, enjoy the relationship you've always wanted with him."

Jalisha peered at Corine. Oh, how much she missed her sister. "You really think so?"

"Yes, I do." She stood to her feet. "Life's too short, Lisha, to hold grudges." She reached out her arms and turned into a full circle. "I'm a prime example of how short life really is." She dropped her hands to her side. "Well, I have to go now. I'll be back to check in on you from time to time, at least for as long as He will allow me."

"I wish you didn't have to go."

"Me, too. I love you."

Jalisha said, "I love you more," and watched Corine fade.

Jalisha stretched her arms above her head, yawned, and wiped the sleep from the corner of her eyes. Her headache was gone. She felt rested and rejuvenated. She knew what she needed to do.

She reached for the phone and dialed Derek.

"Hey, baby," he answered on the first ring. "How are you feeling?"

"Hey, I'm feeling fine. I had a wonderful nap."

"That's good. What's going on with you?"

"I want to talk to you about something."

"What's up?"

"I met my father today."

"Where? That's wonderful, isn't it?"

"At first, I didn't think so, but now I think different. He is a partner at Barlow & Associates."

"Damn, Lisha, he's your boss?"

"Well…yeah, I suppose he is," she chuckled. "He wants to get to know me. What do you think?"

"I think it's great. How do you feel about it?"

"I don't know really. I have mixed emotions. On one hand, I'm excited about finally seeing him face to face and finally have my father in my life. However, on the other hand, I should despise him for never being around."

"Well, tell him. Tell him how you feel about him not being there for you."

"I did, and he said it was Camille who kept him from me."

"I can surely believe that, baby."

"Yeah, I can, too. But he told me he wasn't Corine's father."

"Oh, wow. Well, who is Corine's father?"

She sighed. "It's a long story and not worth getting into."

"So, what are you going to do?"

"I'm going to get to know my father."

"That's my girl." Derek smiled as he sped down I-395.

# *Chapter 45*

Three months had lapsed since Jalisha was reunited with Alfred. She learned he had a wife and she had siblings — a sister and brother — and now, she was seated at his dinner table breaking bread with her new family. For the first time in her life, she felt whole.

"Jalisha, how do you like working at Barlow & Associates?" Alfred's wife, Kathy, asked.

"Surprisingly, I'm really enjoying it."

"Yes, Jalisha is doing extremely well," Alfred interjected.

"Honey, isn't it time for a promotion?" Kathy asked.

"Oh no, I want to advance on my own merit," Jalisha smiled. "Thanks anyway."

"Sweetie, there's nothing wrong with using your father for advancement," Kathy chuckled.

Jalisha smiled as she feasted on pot roast, roasted potatoes, green beans with smoked ham and homemade biscuits.

"You outdid yourself with dinner, Kat," Alfred complimented.

"You're hungry," Kathy chuckled.

"Yes, dinner is very good." Jalisha added, "Where's Chloe and Max?"

Kathy swallowed and took a sip of wine. "Chloe is attending a sleepover with friends and Max is visiting his father."

"His father?"

"Yes," Alfred responded, wiping the creases of his mouth with a white linen napkin. "Max is my stepson. He was three when Kathy and I married. Then, along came Chloe and well, the rest is history."

"How nice." Jalisha smiled enviously. *Why can't this family be my family?*

"So, tell us about Derek."

Jalisha looked at Kathy and said, "Derek is the best thing that's ever happened to me."

"Sounds like someone is in love," Alfred teased.

"Love can be so beautiful," Kathy added. "How about dessert, Jalisha?"

"No, thank you."

"You sure? I have homemade sweet potato pie."

"Sure, I'll have a sliver," she said, forcing a smile. She absolutely hated sweet potato pie. "A thin piece, Kathy. You know a girl is trying to watch her figure."

"So what does Derek do for a living?" Alfred asked as he sawed into his pot roast.

"He develops computer systems."

"Where did he go to school?"

"I don't know," Jalisha answered with the same forced smile.

"Didn't he go to college?" Alfred asked.

Jalisha peered at Alfred with annoyance at his inquisition. "I don't know if he went to college. I never asked him."

"You would want someone with a college degree."

"What does a college degree have to do with how he treats me, Alfred?" she asked sternly.

"A college degree will ensure he can take care of you," Alfred implied.

"I don't need him to take care of me," she snapped. She was getting pissed. How dare he question her about anything, especially when he's only been in her life a hot minute?

"I'm sure your father didn't mean it that way," Kathy said, trying to douse the potential flame that was brewing inside Jalisha.

"No, I know exactly what he meant." She turned her attention toward Alfred. "Don't talk about Derek like he is beneath you, because he's not. He's more man than you are. If it weren't for Derek and Corine, I wouldn't be sitting here eating your food and digesting your bullshit!"

Alfred tossed his napkin onto his plate. "Wait a minute, Jalisha," he snapped in an authoritative tone. "If I've offended you, I do apologize. But you will not disrespect me at my table and in my own house. I don't tolerate disrespect from my other children, and I won't tolerate it from you."

"Enough," Kathy scolded them. "Alfred, yes you are Jalisha's father, but you are not in the position to question who she dates."

"I'm not questioning anything. I'm only making an observation."

"You can keep your observations to yourself," Kathy snapped, obviously fed up with the unnecessary bickering between Jalisha and Alfred. "Baby, you can't jump into the father role as if nothing happened. Honey, years have passed by. Try being her friend. You don't want to start out as her enemy."

Alfred leaned back in his chair, rested his hands on the arms of the chair, and grunted. "You're right, Kat."

Kathy smiled and turned toward Jalisha. "Sweetie, you aren't any better. I understand the bitterness you may be harboring, but you have to give also. Give him a chance. Give yourself a chance."

Jalisha allowed Kathy's words to digest. She was happy finally to have her father in her life, but she wanted to make sure the ground rules were laid and understood. After all, she was a grown woman. Alfred missed her childhood, which was by no account of his own.

Jalisha faced Alfred and gazed into her reflection. She was the spitting image of her father. The nose, eyes, lips and, as she'd recognized, the disposition were all a mirror image. "I'm sorry, Alfred...I mean, Dad."

Alfred's eyes lit up like shooting stars and boy, did they grow in size.

"Wonderful," Kathy sang. "It's time to become a family."

# *Chapter 46*

Three months had passed. Jalisha was enjoying her newfound relationship with Alfred. Her love for Derek grew by the minute. This was her life, as she knew it. The only one missing was Corine. She hadn't had a visit from Corine in quite some time. Maybe it was a sign her life was on the right track.

Jalisha smiled as she reminisced on the days she and Corine would hunch down behind the door and watch Camille work hard for her money. "Yeah, right," she murmured.

"What's that?" Derek asked.

"Nothing," she smiled.

Derek and Jalisha were spending their usual Sunday morning at her place. Jalisha sat indulging a cup of herbal tea, while Derek sipped on vanilla chai. Vivaldi's The Four Seasons danced around, as they lay intertwined on the sofa, him with the newspaper and her with the latest issue of O Magazine.

"I love her hair," Jalisha commented.

"Who?" Derek asked with his face buried deep into the business section of The Washington Post.

"Oprah. She has bouncing and behaving hair."

"You would too if you paid a stylist to style it everyday."

"I wish I had Oprah's money. Humph, you wouldn't be able to tell me shit."

"No one can tell you shit now," he chuckled.

Jalisha kicked the paper with her foot. "Kiss my ass, Derek."

Derek puckered his lips. "I'm down with the program."

Jalisha rolled her eyes and pulled herself up from the sofa.

"Where are you going?"

"I'm hungry," she answered, heading toward the kitchen.

"Babe, we ate an hour ago."

"I know and I'm feeling hungry again."

Derek lowered the paper and affixed his eyes to his woman's round voluptuous bottom. After all these months, it still gave him goose bumps. However, it looked fuller than usual.

"Babe, are you putting on weight?"

Jalisha peeked around the corner. "Why would you ask me that? What are you trying to say?"

"Whoa! Down, girl. Don't go getting in a huff. I'm only making an observation. Besides, I like your ass the way it is." Derek tried to smooth things over, but it was too late. He'd already hit the sore spot.

Jalisha had noticed lately how her clothes were fitting her snug. She had put on a few pounds, but she attributed the extra pounds to them going out to dinner five days a week. However, her healthy appetite of late didn't help either.

"Lish, did you get your period?"

Jalisha soaked up Derek's question and tried to remember the last time she had a period. After their first month of deciding to be exclusive, the condoms never saw the light of day again.

"That's a good question," she said, plopping on the sofa with her hand nestled inside a bag of Doritos. "I'm out of Pepsi. Could you run down to the 7-11 and get me one?"

"Anything else you want?"

"Nope, that's it."

Derek slipped on his slippers and headed for the door.

"I know you are not going out with bedroom slippers on."

"Why not? I'm going down the street."

"Go on with your ghetto ass," she chuckled.

Jalisha's attention turned to Essence Magazine. Derek had turned her on to Iyanla Vanzant. She admired her tell-it-like-it-is attitude and her wisdom. Now, every month, she made sure to purchase a copy of Essence so she could read what Iyanla had to say. This month's "Ask Iyanla" dealt with delinquent dads. Touché, she thought.

When the door closed behind Derek, Jalisha leapt from the sofa and darted down the hall toward the bedroom. She made a beeline to her nightstand and pulled out her monthly calendar. During her years of prostitution, she had formed a habit of keeping track of her monthly. Although she was avid when it came to condoms, and never left the house without a stash, her biggest fear was ending up pregnant by a faceless being. Quickly, she flipped to the current month, nothing. She wrote nothing down. She flipped back to the previous month, nothing. Frantically, she flipped two months ago and not a scribble.

"Damn, damn, damn!" she blurted out.

She returned the calendar to the nightstand drawer. Suddenly feeling queasy, she sat on the edge of the bed and held on to her stomach.

Me, a mother? This can't be, she thought. I don't know how to be a mother.

Thoughts of abortion flashed through her mind until Derek stormed through the door.

"Hey baby, got your Pepsi. They didn't have vanilla, so I got the regular Pepsi."

A smile formed across Jalisha's lips. A baby is what Derek always wanted and, God willing, a baby is what he'd have.

She went into the living room and sat down beside Derek. "Thanks for the Pepsi, baby."

"No problem," he smiled, resuming his reading position.

Jalisha wasn't quite sure how she was going to tell Derek she may or may not be pregnant. Should she wait until after she had a pregnancy test? If she were pregnant, though, she would want him included in every step. like those EPT commercials, she would want them to both look at the stick and cry tears of joy together.

"The answer to your question is no," she said, her eyes nailed to his face. She wanted to see his expression more than anything else. Would he be happy?

Derek flipped through the sections of the newspaper. "What question?" he asked, not taking his eyes off the newspaper, enthralled at the small letters before him.

"No, I didn't get my period yet."

He paused. He raised his head, and his eyes met with hers. "You're pregnant?"

"Maybe, I don't know. It could be possible."

Derek grinned from ear to ear.

"So you would be happy?"

"Are you kidding me? I'd be ecstatic!" Derek jumped to his feet and pulled her up to face him. "Baby, this is a dream come true." He twirled her around and locked his lips with hers, tasting the mixture of Doritos and herbal tea. "Baby, I love you so much! Do you know what this means?"

Jalisha looked puzzled. "It means we are going to have a baby, maybe."

With Jalisha's hand in his, Derek dropped down to one knee. He looked up at her and said, "Jalisha Thomas, I've loved you from the first time I laid eyes on you."

"Oh my God, Derek," she whimpered, trying to hold back the tears of joy.

"Jalisha, make me the happiest man on earth. Marry me."

Jalisha's mouth fell open, her bottom lip dangled toward the floor. Tears flowed from her eyes like a never-ending waterfall.

"Yes, Derek, I'll marry you," she whispered.

Derek stood to his feet and wrapped her in his arms.

Jalisha buried her head into his chest, deeply inhaled his scent, and thanked God for all of his blessings.

# *Chapter 47*

Nine months later, Jalisha and Derek became proud parents of a beautiful baby girl they named Grace Corine. Three months later, Jalisha and Derek were married…in the cemetery before Corine's gravesite, as Kathy, Alfred, Chloe and Max stood by their side. Corine was there too, as well as Camille. Looks like Corine found her after all.

"She seems quite happy," Corine smiled.

Camille placed her arm around Corine's shoulder. "Yes, she does,"she cried as she witnessed Jalisha and Derek exchange vows.

"Isn't Grace Corine beautiful? She looks just like Jalisha too."

Camille wiped her nose with the back of her hand. "Yes, she is beautiful."

"I never knew Daddy was so handsome."

"Hmph," Camille shrugged. "He's all right."

Corine chuckled and glanced at Camille. "Mom, why are you crying? This is a happy occassion."

"Oh, I'm very happy for my baby. She's come quite a distance, hurdling every obstacle placed before her."

"So why are you crying?"

Camille caressed Corine by the hand and held it close to her heart. "Because, Corey, the apple fell from the tree, rolled down the hill and has planted firmly in the ground."

# Apple Tree

Corine embraced Camille and kissed her on the cheek. "I love you, Mom."

"I love you too, baby."

COMING
Christmas 2004!!

The Anticipated Sequel to
*Anything Goes!!*

*The Sweet Taste of*

*Revenge*

*A Novel*
*Jessica Tilles*

Dear Reader:

To everyone who sent emails, instant messages, stopped me in the grocery store, interrupted my dinner dates (trust me, some of those dates needed to be interrupted), and attended my signings (a quick shout out to Bruce Pugh — Raven is still going strong), you know not what you've asked for. Can you handle a sequel? Remember, hell hath no fury like a woman scorned.

Chances are you've already read *Anything Goes*. If not, you're in for a treat. However, in order for you to completely understand what makes Raven tick, you must read *Anything Goes*. So, don't hesitate. Pick up your copy of *Anything Goes* so you'll be well prepared to handle *The Sweet Taste of Revenge.*

Order *Anything Goes* and other titles by me, using the order form in the back, and receive 20% off. Inquire about bulk purchases at xypublishing@aol.com.

Lastly, my mailbox is always opened. Please feel free to email me at JTilles@AOL.com with your thoughts.

Sit back, kick up your feet, better grab a glass of something strong because you're going to need it, and enjoy Chapter 1 of *The Sweet Taste of Revenge*.

Always,

Jessica Gilles

# *Chapter 1*

Sweat glistened on Ramone's bruised naked body. His wrists and ankles were secured to the four-poster bed, as Raven drilled into his rectum vigorously and frequently. Her strap-on dildo had become an extension of her being. The role of dominatrix felt natural to her and took her higher than a Philly blunt busting at the seams with marijuana laced with crack. She felt an addiction coming on.

A wicked grin crossed her lips as she hung up the phone. "Good boy," she said, patting Ramone on the top of his head, just like a raggedy ass dog. "Now, while we are waiting for your whorish ass wife, who likes to pick up married men in bars, I'm going to take a shower. The smell of you makes me want to puke," she lashed out, her venom more poisonous than a snake.

"Ray, aren't you going to untie me?"

Raven looked over her shoulder and smirked. "Do I look like a fucking fool to you?"

"Please Ray. I'm in so much pain."

"Good!"

"Please Ray."

She faced him and leaned against the wall with her arms folded across her chest. "Ramone, I don't give a rat's ass if you're in pain."

"You crazy bitch, I was good to you. Why are you doing this?"

She strolled toward the satchel bag sitting next to the nightstand and retrieved the .22-caliber from its holster. She had no intentions of using the gun. She merely wanted to scare the shit out of him.

Ramone's eyes widened and flooded with fear and tears.

She squatted down before him. "Ramone, did you really think you could get away with lying to me?"

"Ray, please don't kill me," he cried. "I was wrong for not telling you about Renee, but I didn't think it would've made a difference. You said you only wanted the dick and nothing more," he pleaded for his life.

"Ramone, you hurt me. I gave myself to you for three years. You did things to me I would've never allowed anyone to do to me. You brought another man into my home to fuck me while you watched."

"But, I thought it was what you wanted?"

"It was and I enjoyed it immensely, which is why I am fucking your boy, Chas."

"Fuck Chas."

She waved her index finger in his face. "Ooh, that's not very nice of you, Ramone."

"Man, why did he have to go and tap my pussy?"

"Don't blame this shit on Chas. After all, you're the one who led the horse to the water. He simply took a drink."

"He will never be me," he snarled, his body heaving with anger.

"You're right, once again. Chas will never be like you because he has what you don't."

"Yeah, and what's that?"

"Me," she smiled as she eyed Ramone's body. Oh how she loved sexing him. He did things to her that made her toes and hair curl. But, he had to mess it up by not telling her he was married. As far as she was concerned, Ramone was no different than Jay, the no good bastard who jilted her at the altar.

Thoughts of Jay took her back to Marcy's apartment. She winced. She used a dildo then too. What was becoming of her fascinations with dildos?

"Bitch, you are old news," he snapped, breaking her trance. "Yeah, I had my way with you. I fucked you when and where I wanted. You're the dumb bitch for allowing me to do it to your ass."

Raven's brow raised in fury. "I *suggest* you *shut* the fuck up," she spoke between clinched teeth.

Not heading her words, he continued, "Yeah, I did what the fuck I wanted to do to you," he cackled. "Remember the time I made you get on your knees and suck my dick in a pissy ass alley in Anacostia? Uh huh, and since we're going back down memory lane, remember the time I took you over to my boy's crib and the fellas ran a train on your freak nasty ass?" His laughter was uncontrollable, reminiscent of the Joker from Batman & Robin.

She slowly stood up. "Yes, I remember," she whispered, as she hovered over him. Ramone's mouth had pushed her to the edge. If he wasn't careful, she wouldn't be responsible for her next move.

"Yeah, I fucked your ass royally and you loved it. The only difference between you and those tricks on 14th and U Streets is you do it for free, you dumb bitch!" he spat in her face, leaving her with the burning desire to end his life.

Raven's hand wrapped tightly around the cold, black metal as beads of sweat formed on her forehead.

"Chas can have your used up ass. Your shit's been stretched so wide, it's like the fucking black hole." He laughed in hysterically in her face. "You used to be tight, now my dick gets lost up in ya!"

Ramone's words stung deep and the blood running through her veins was at its boiling point. Her hands shook and her knees weakened. She felt like she was on shaky ground. She felt queasy, her breathing turned into short pants. Nevertheless, she maintained her cool.

"Anything else you need to get off your chest, baby?" she asked reaching for the pillow lying beside Ramone's bruised head.

Ramone's laughter was hard and uncontrollable. He could barely speak. "Yeah, does Arthur know you and Morgan swap pussy juices?"

Ramone went for the jugular. He attacked the one person in her life who meant the world to her. He demeaned her sister in one breath. Was he stupid?

She placed the pillow over his head.

Ramone knew his fate, but he had to say one last thing. "Raven, I love you."

His body jolted and went limp from the muffled gun shot to the back of his head. Blood splattered against the headboard. A collage of red spots and streaks painted the white cotton sheets.

"Look at what you made me do," she said to the blood stained pillow. "I told you to stop running your mouth."

Morgan's words played over and over in her head, haunting her. *Ray, it is time for you to stand up and take responsibility for your own actions. I don't care how you do it, but you need to do it and do it without me. Ray, you don't think about anyone but yourself.*

"Stop, stop, stop!" she yelled, her palms plastered to her ears. "Leave me alone!"

Ready for a straight jacket, Raven took deep breaths and tried to gather her composure. She needed to clean the place up. What was she going to do with the body? She cased the room with her eyes. She thought back to the night she and Morgan were at Marcy's apartment. She ran to the bathroom, grabbed a towel and dampened it with hot, soapy water. She wiped down everything she touched, from the bed, to the nightstand, to the doorknobs. She gathered her belongings and the sheets from the bed. Where was she going to put the comforter? She looked in the closet for one of those plastic bags you use to put your dirty clothes in, neatly folded the comforter and shoved it inside the plastic bag. It wasn't a perfect fit, but it served the purpose.

She stood in the middle of the room, looked around and confirmed she had cleaned every surface. However, she felt she had missed something. Then it dawned on her. She had touched Ramone's clothes. She snatched his clothes from the tattered burnt orange-colored chair and shoved them into her satchel.

As she proceeded to the door, a knock stopped her in her tracks.

She contemplated whether she should answer the knock. She desperately wanted to vacate the room. Being so close to Ramone's dead body was making her heave up the turkey sandwich she had for lunch.

The knock is persistent.

"Ramone, its Renee," came from the other side of the door.

"Oh shit," she mouthed.

Raven slowly tip toed to the door and looked through the peephole. She stood behind the door and opened it slowly.

"Ramone?" Renee walked through the door with caution. "Where are…," the sight of her husband's dead body stopped her in her tracks. "Oh my, God. . .Ramone!" She ran to his side as Raven slammed the door behind her, startling her.

Raven stood before her enemy. "Hello Renee." She walked toward the bed. "Well, you finally made it. You almost missed me."

Renee took her stare off Ramone's corpse and directed it toward Raven. "Did you do this?"

"Naw, he did it to himself." She dropped her hands to her side. "He was a bad boy and he had to be punished."

Renee stood in shock, her eyes moving from Raven, to the door, to the phone. She looked confused.

"If I were you, I would think twice about reaching for the phone or the door. My level of tolerance is very low, as you can see." She pointed to Ramone's corpse.

"But I don't understand."

"Sure you do. You understand fully. From what I hear, you know all about me."

Renee looked like she'd seen a ghost. "Raven Ward?"

"It ain't Memorex, honey."

"Huh?"

"Listen, the way I see it, you have three choices. One, I can keep you alive and spend the rest of my life behind bars for killing your two-timing husband, but we don't want that." Raven pulled the .22-caliber from the satchel and walked around the bed to where Renee stood. "Two, I can have you lie face down beside him, place a pillow over your head and you two can spend the rest of eternity in hell." She picked up a pillow. "Three, I can have you lie face up on the bed, place the pillow over your face and shoot you in the head, then place the gun in your hand and call it a murder suicide," Raven smiled, followed by a slight chuckle.

"You are a crazy bitch!" Renee exclaimed, wringing her hands together.

"That's what Ramone said."

"You will never get away with this."

"Yada, yada, yada, what will it be, one, two or three?"

"I prefer four," Renee shouted as she kicked her right leg toward Raven's face, attempting to knock the gun from her hand. Unfortunately, she lost her footing, slipped and knocked her head against the corner of the oak-carved nightstand and fell unconscious.

Raven looked down at Renee with a questionable look. "Oh, you're trying to be Jackie Chan on a sister, huh?"

Raven grabbed Renee by her weave and lifted her to the bed, lying her face up beside her beloved Ramone. She wrinkled up her nose at the smell of intercourse around Renee's mouth and lower extremities. She placed the pillow over her face. "Enjoy hell, bitch," she snarled as she pulled the trigger, firing a muffled gunshot to the side of Renee's head.

She used soap and water to wipe down the gun and placed it in Renee's hand. She removed the pillowcases and shoved them into her satchel, not leaving much room for anything else. As she left the room, she thought, *it was a good thing I purchased the gun hot off the street. Who knows whom it's registered to?*

She opened the door. With her back to the hallway, she took one last glance over the room. When she closed the door, she turned and came face-to-face with Arthur.

"Raven, what have you done?"

"What business is it of yours?"

"Where are Renee and Ramone?"

"Oh, so now you are concerned about Renee? I thought you wanted her out of the picture, Arthur?"

"Well, yes, but I didn't want any harm to come to her either."

"Ha! It's too late for that, babe."

"What do you mean?"

"You shouldn't have fucked her, Arthur!"

"I didn't…"

"Yes you did! She reeked of cum! You sonofabitch! Did you think to use a fucking condom?

"Open the door, Raven," he ordered.

"Arthur, I suggest you turn yourself around and go home to your wife, where you belong. It's your fault I did what I did."

"How is it my fault?"

She grabbed him by the crotch. "You gave up my dick and I thought we had an understanding."

"Listen, Raven…"

"No, you listen. You will go home to your wife, be the loving husband you've always been and you will keep your dick in check and never, ever do this shit again. I will go home, shower, relax and call Chas."

"So we are over?" Excitement danced in his voice.

"Oh hell no, sugar. You see, Morgan spoke so highly of the size of your dick and of your ability to perform in the bedroom, I wanted to fuck. She wasn't lying, you do have a big dick and you are very good. Morgan and I share so much, why not you? Go home."

# Novels by *Jessica Tilles*

_____ *Anything Goes*, ISBN: 0-9722990-0-9
$12.00* (Reg. $15.00)

_____ *In My Sisters' Corner*, ISBN: 0-9722990-1-7
$12.00* (Reg. $15.00)

_____ *Apple Tree*, ISBN: 0-9722990-2-5
$12.00* (Reg. $15.00)

Maryland residents, add 5% sales tax to your order.

**Send to:**
Xpress Yourself Publishing
P.O. Box 1615
Upper Marlboro, MD 20773

Please send me the books I have checked above. I am enclosing $_____ (plus 5% sales tax for Maryland residents). Send check or money order — no cash or C.O.D.s please.  Allow up to two weeks for delivery.

Name _____

Address _____

City _____State/Zip _____

Autograph to _____

*Offer valid using this order form only. Offer not valid at www.jessicatilles.com or bookstores.        AT-1